STEEL SOLDIER: VAGABONDS

Oliver Salvas

1

Victor slept soundly in his bunk aboard the interstellar battleship the *Hummingbird*. The room was a pale gray with smooth, blank walls. The very few possessions that he owned were piled up neatly in a nightstand to the left of his bunk. The bunk was made into the wall, conserving floor space. It felt like a coffin. A very dim light strip steadily increased in brightness as the motion detectors picked up on Victor stirring in his bed

With almost a week to go before his first combat drop, he wanted to get as much rest as possible. Victor might have been a soldier, but he wasn't free of his emotions. He was still scared. Serge, his bunk mate and commanding officer, burst through the door and turned on a desk lamp. He threw Victor's uniform at him and tore the blanket off of the sleeping rookie. The black uniform whipped against Victor's face. A red stripe down each arm met over his heart where his squad's emblem was sewn in. A snarling panther in front of the moon.

Serge's face was aged well beyond his actual age. The constant battle and the brutal training regime he put himself through was evident on his face, but also his body. He was built like a loading suit. His muscles refused to be soft. His hair was starting to gray and he always had a thick stubble of beard that he only shaved for meetings with high ranking officers. The stubble helped cover the scars and burns he accumulated throughout the years of battle.

"Let's go kid, did they not teach you that there's a strict schedule a week before a drop?" Victor groaned and rubbed the sleep from his eyes. He sat up and grimaced at Serge. "Also hurry the hell up, drop week has all the best food, it'll be a warzone in there."

"I had an alarm set ten minutes from now," Victor mumbled, "why didn't you let me sleep in until then?"

"Because you have to wake up at exactly eight in the morning: drop zone standard time. If you don't like the Prol Intergalactic Alliance standards, just write a letter to the Triumvirate representatives." Victor blinked and slowly stumbled out of bed. He put on his uniform, a black jumpsuit with a single red stripe down each limb.

Serge was already out the door and into the hallway before Victor made himself look presentable enough to be regarded as a special forces member. He caught up to Serge with a brisk walk. The smooth gray halls quickly became flooded as every crew member woke up, got dressed, and headed to the mess hall for breakfast. Decorations in the hallways of the *Hummingbird* were as few as in Victor's room. An occasional screen showed pictures of soldiers in triumphant poses with smiles on their faces or stunning naturescapes that could be ruined by war in minutes. It was easy to tell who the rookies were. They were either barely awake, way too awake, or being dragged out of their rooms by their bunk mates.

As Victor and Serge raced to the dining hall, they passed a wide variety of different soldiers. Many wore the drap gray of the Iron Corps, standard foot soldiers. A few bright colors dotted the wave of gray. Victor recognized some of the other special squads. He recalled the names of the White Camels, Indigo Hawks, Daylight Otters, and the Blood Scorpions.

When the two arrived, there was already a line almost all the way around the hall, with murmuring from all different divisions and stations filling the room.

Serge was one of the oldest people among the soldiers. This meant that he could cut in line during dining hours, not out of seniority, but out of respect. Serge was a veteran of seven years, since the beginning of the Kross uprising.

The Kross uprising turned the galaxy into the largest civil war known to humanity. With the growing need for soldiers, the Prol have turned to genetic breeding. Every soldier is bred to be in the best rank that the genetic donors' DNA can get them. Not every soldier lives up to those high expectations. Soldiers that fail to meet those expectations are drafted into the Iron Corps. Most members of the Iron Corps don't last two battles, but those that do can earn their way back into Steel Corps, or more commonly known as the Steel Soldiers.

The Prol Intergalactic Alliance, often shortened to simply the Prol, consists of an uneasy alliance of the three remaining superpowers from a long past civil war. The alliance is governed by an unknown trio known as the Triumvirate. They make the laws, rename planets as they see fit, and even repurpose planets for the good of humanity. Without the Prol, humanity would fall to a chaotic rabble, so say the Triumvirate.

Steel Soldiers are the best the Prol can put on the battlefield. Every Steel Soldier has an ARJAC finely tuned for their exact needs. ARJACs are Armored Joint-Axis Cores, humanoid tanks with the destructive power of a small army. They can be configured for any kind of combat, such as sniping, covert ops, and front line combat. Defeating an ARJAC is a near suicidal feat for anyone besides another Steel Soldier.

Serge squeezed into the line and dragged Victor along with him. They each pressed their shoulders against the check-in terminal mounted on the wall.

Good morning Victor, today I recommend eating more than usual. It is one week before a combat drop and it is ill-advised to train without the proper caloric intake.

The A.I. implant in Victor's shoulder transmitted directly into his brain. "Thanks Arjie" Victor retorted. Serge gave him a sideways glance.

"Why did you give it a nickname? Also you know only you can hear it right?"

Victor nudged Serge, "What's the fun if I can't be friends with something I'm stuck with for life?" Serge shook his head and got a plateful of hash browns and sausage.

Every Steel Soldier is required to have an A.I. implanted in them to assist in piloting their ARJAC.

The A.I. handles the background tasks so the pilot can focus on the battle in front of them. In case the ARJAC is destroyed and the pilot isn't, the A.I. also comes with the knowledge of basic survival and communications techniques. Due to the innovations of the Prol Intergalactic Alliance, ARJACs and Steel Soldiers are interchangeable, any ARJAC can be piloted by any Steel Soldier, however the results of doing so vary wildly. The A.I. learns and adapts with each soldier. It learns the best ways to transfer information and pilot the ARJAC to the Steel Soldier's preferences. Drop week is used as a last minute preparation for the A.I. to understand how the soldier wants to fight with their current mentality.

Serge and Victor found the other two members of their special unit known as The Nightcats. A number of empty and half-full plates littered the respectably sized tabletop. Sausages, breakfast sandwiches, and a few fruit skins lay casually tossed aside on plates pushed away from the owner. Kali greeted Serge with a casual "Sir," and a smile to Victor. Rutri continued to look out into deep space, disregarding their arrival.

Nightcat-Lead, shortened to simply Cat Lead, is Serge. Serge fought in too many battles to count. Serge was present when the Prol won back planets such as Demeter-4, a paradise world for government officials, and Plutus-11, an agricultural world that still hasn't recovered. He pilots a general combat welterweight ARJAC, suited for every encounter, and just as deadly in each one. It features an array of communications and command suites.

Cat-2 is Kali. Her face radiates warmth even in the

cold depths of space. Her long dark hair was put up in a tight military bun. Her supporting fire role makes her the ideal second in command. She has saved Serge and every previous member of Nightcat squad on more than a few occasions with her pinpoint accuracy. Her cruiserweight ARJAC has little armor, but can rain hell upon an army from any range. Its armaments consist of a heavy Gauss cannon, long range missiles, a backup gauss rifle, and the standard head mounted machine guns.

The heavy armaments role, Rutri, is Cat-3. His ARJAC is considered cruiserweight. His ARJAC is generally deployed with dual Gr-1 Gauss Rifles, a generous missile salvo, and a bludgeon for good measure. Rutri is the other rookie in the Nightcats. His brute strength mentality during exercises caught the attention of Serge, earning him a place among the Nightcats. His body's small frame has led to a number of people being beaten in training due to underestimating his abilities as a pilot.

Victor takes the Cat-4 slot as the Bantamweight scout. Victor's ARJAC is specially fitted for hit-and-run style tactics, reconnaissance, and flanking. With light armor, light weapons, and some of the fastest legs in the galaxy, very few can keep up. Victor's initial tests of reaction time broke facility records, leading him to become the top guerrilla fighter in his class. His ARJAC is only equipped with a small missile salvo, and a lighter version of the GR-1, called a GR-1s.

The two sat down and ate. Kali inspected Serge's tray with an over the top gesture, gave an approving nod, and then turned to Victor's. She shook her head and picked a sausage from the tray. "You know, too much meat will slow you down Victor." She continued with a mouthful of sausage, "You need those speedy quick reflexes! How are you going to train properly this way? You might even gain some weight!"

Serge chuckled and Rutri groaned. Victor shook his head, grinning. "I won't gain weight! Have you *seen* Serge's training regimen? I'd be lucky to have any body fat left when we drop."

An Iron Corps soldier strutted up to their table. She clearly looked eager to talk, seemingly comfortable enough after she saw the body language of the squad. The sausage stealing stopped and everyone looked at her, confused. "Is there something I can help you with, Corporal?" Serge looked her over. Her green and gray uniform was not in great condition, but certainly not in bad condition either. Her light hair was cut short. She looked like she had seen only minutes of real combat.

"You guys are Steel Soldiers right? Do you have any stories to tell about battles or anything? I might be able to learn a thing or two!" Her voice sounded a lot less confident than her walk. Serge raised an eyebrow. She paused for a second. "Sir."

Serge nodded, he had earned that respect. "Let me think." He stroked his stubble as if it was a magnificent beard. "Have I ever told the story of the Battle of Vivaldre?"

"Several times, yes, and it's boring as hell." Rutri butted in.

"Oh shush, I love this one!" Kali eagerly awaited to hear it for the who-knows-how-many time.

Serge clapped once and tugged the soldier's sleeve to sit down. "Have you ever been married soldier?"

She shook her head, confused by the notion of marriage. "It's against Prol law for soldiers to marry."

"Well this ones gonna be a wild ride so buckle up and be prepared to be scolded for being late to duties," Serge started. "I'm sure you've heard about the battle countless times, but what about after?"

Serge told the story about how after the Battle of Vivaldre had ended there were no available shuttles to extract Kali and himself. The battle on the planet had been won by the Prol, but the battle in Space had been a supreme Kross victory. The two had to go into hiding for months until the Kross were eventually defeated by the Prol reinforcements. Until then, Serge and Kali found a small village which had been untouched by the devastation. They hid their ARJACs in a nearby cave and assimilated into the village under the cover of refugees.

At this point in the story Rutri went to get more food, mumbling the whole way there and back. Kali slapped him on the arm and shushed him. The soldier was hanging on to every word.

The small hamlet was a very traditional village and the only way for a man and woman to live together was to be married. Being married is against Prol military standards, so there was no "real wedding," or so says the report. Months passed before Prol shuttles were seen descending from space. Serge and Kali quickly left under the cover of night and boarded their ARJACs to signal for a pickup.

"Any longer down there and we might have had a kid!" Kali laughed. "I'm kidding!" She gave a jovial smile.

The soldier was speechless for a moment. After thinking over the story and comparing it to others she had heard she spoke up, "I've heard about the battle so many times but no one wants to speak about what happened after. It seems you two got lucky with that village. It was hell for most of the survivors."

"Tell that to the other two Nightcats" Rutri sat back down at the table and resumed looking out the window, occasionally eating another forkful of food.

The five ate in awkward silence for the last few minutes. Serge eventually stood up, stretched, and put his hands on the table. "Alright breakfast is over! Nightcats, it's time for morning routines! Young lady, I suggest you head back over to your designated area." The Iron Corps soldier hurried away after giving a quick salute and a bow of thanks.

The Nightcats trained every day, for as long as it took to learn every scenario inside and out. Every possible thing that could go wrong was practiced over and over, until minimal damage was sustained. Then they redid all those scenarios on different terrain. The training pods were practically burnt out by the end of the week. Off-duty duels were held among the Steel Soldiers of every company participating in the drop. Duels were encouraged because the soldiers trained for any one-on-one combat they might encounter. The officers oversee the bets and tournaments that take place, since it keeps the moral up.

Victor decided to enter the tournament. His second fight was against Rutri. They agreed on hand to hand combat with minimal ranged weapons using simulated Welterweight ARJACs. Victor had wanted to beat Rutri at his own game. The rules were to neutralize the opponent however possible. First to two wins advances to the next stage. The arena of choice for this tournament was the exact opposite of the Moon of Jenrika, their soon-to-be war zone. The virtual arena was a lush forest with towering trees and birds that flew into the virtual display cameras. Lush underbrush sometimes snagged on the feet of the ARJACs, causing them to stumble or fall over.

The first round, Victor stood his ground and was ripped to shreds by Rutri's melee prowess. The second round Victor tried to implement some kind of strategy. He decided to attack quickly, guessing Rutri's first move would be the same as the first round. Victor managed to get a right hook right into the head of Rutri's ARJAC, causing temporary viewfinder malfunctions and major stability loss. Rutri swung blindly, but Victor deftly danced around him, sweeping his legs and stomping his head, winning against Rutri.

The third round was the most boring to watch for the spectators, but the most heart pounding fight Victor had ever experienced. He knew he couldn't get lucky like he did in round two. The second the timer marked the start of the round, Victor turned and dashed into the forest. Hoping to lure Rutri in, he peppered Rutri with grazing fire from his machine guns. He waited within the trees after clearing visual sight. The radar blipped as Rutri came into range. Victor quickly shut down his ARJAC to stop appearing on Rutri's radar. Rutri would know his general location, so he'd have to act fast, and on pure intuition.

He waited in silence for an unknown length of time. It could have been hours for all he knew. He ran every possibility in his head. "Would he sprint towards me? Will he be more cautious? Is he already here? How many seconds has it been? I retreated for a minute but it didn't take him long to catch up. If only the simulator would tell me ground tremors. Does it tell me the ground tremors?" He paused, inspecting his virtual sensors. "Definitely no ground tremors."

Victor turned his ARJAC back on. The viewfinder flickered on and Rutri's ARJAC stood right in front of him, winding up for the biggest, most powerful strike possible. Victor put his arms up as quickly as he could to guard, but Rutri's punch shattered Victor's wrists, causing sparks to fly everywhere and knocking his head clean off.

Victor opened the simulator hatch to an ocean of jeers for putting on such a boring show during the third round. Kali patted him on the back. "At least you had the right mindset. Kinda." Victor shrugged off her hand. "Hey and next time, remember that simulators are only so realistic. You might've had him if that was a real fight. I doubt that strategy would fly with Serge though, way too risky."

"Thanks Kali, but now I won't be able to afford any souvenirs when we get there. They barely pay me as it is. I bet most of my upcoming pay on that match."

"Ask Rutri to buy you something, since he has your money now." Kali laughed. Rutri unceremoniously climbed down and received his portion of the bets that he had placed. He gave a sly smile and thumbs up to Victor.

The rest of the tournament went without any more boring tactics. Serge won second place only because he decided to face Kali in a sniper duel. Kali threw the first round to give a good show to the crowds. "Who doesn't like the underdog getting some hope?" She said afterwards.

The Nightcats had too many rounds of drinks that night. Everyone did, but the Nightcats had more of a reason, since almost all of them made it to the finals of the gladiatorial tournament. The next morning was rough for the entire ship, breakfast was so quiet the only sounds were soldiers loading their plates with food, trying to eat off their collective hangover mixed with groans from pounding headaches.

Victor collected his usual breakfast plate, sat down at the usual table, and put his head down. He suddenly remembered that tomorrow he'll be on a foreign planet, fighting strange people for a cause he didn't fully understand. He gagged, paused and forced breakfast down. Victor may have been passed out all night, but his dreams were vivid and racked full of what the future could hold for him. He kept dreaming of his demise at the end of a Gauss Rifle. What if a well placed tank shell penetrated his armor? He couldn't stop the onslaught of dreams.

Then came drop day. The Nightcats were slated to drop at 1700 hours, local time of the continent on Jenrika. Their objective was to locate one of the two mining facilities on the small moon. Prol intelligence suggested that one of the facilities is actually a secret ARJAC factory for the Kross rebels. Another team that was on the *Hummingbird* had been assigned to the other facility.

"So that ends our official briefing Nightcats!" Serge flicked off the hologram projector showing Mining Facility Bravo. "Any questions?"

Victor raised his hand in the dark, spacious room, "So who's going to Mining Facility Alpha, Sir?"

"Since it's going to be a lot brighter on their side of the moon, command decided to go with the White Camels, I'm sure you've seen them walking around." Serge motioned for Victor to complete the statement about the White Camels, testing his knowledge.

"They're an artillery specialty unit. They recently earned clearance for a BOB." Victor stated with slight hesitation. He had overheard some of the Iron Corps soldiers talking about it a few days ago.

Serge flicked on the projector again and typed into the console. A bulky six-legged platform similar to an oversized tank appeared. An artillery cannon that reached from stern to bow stretched into the upper levels of the holographic projector.

"BOBs are Battlefield Operation Behemoths, in some off chance you didn't know that. Most of the time they are used as something like a mobile base of operations for when the area is still hot. The White Camels are an artillery specialty unit, so that means this big bastard has an upscaled matter cannon that can take out a cruiser in one shot. If we pay attention we might feel it today during the operation."

Rutri silently nodded with approval at the immense firepower. Serge turned off the projector again. "We have a few hours before drop time, you're all free to do whatever until then. Just keep an eye on the time."

The three stood and saluted Serge, turned sharply, and walked out. Serge sighed in the empty room. As he was walking out the door Kali poked her head from around the corner. He gave her a weary smile.

"Any plans until drop time sir?" Kali gave her best deep voiced soldier impression. She finished her question with a light chuckle, realizing how strange she sounded.

"I was planning on just trying to avoid people," Serge shrugged. "I'm not a fan of these high altitude drops, they always make me sick." He leaned on the projector's frame, remembering how many times he had to deal with vomit in his cockpit.

"Well then let's avoid people together! I'm not so much a fan of these big drops either. I have to clean up all the cute little trinkets in my cockpit every time we do one."

"Have you ever thought about gluing them down

or something? Definitely couldn't hurt to try," He mimed glueing a small object.

"Serge, you know I like to move them around from time to time. It's really the only thing that I have control over in this crazy galaxy." Kali's cockpit collection has become a token of good luck for her, as well as anyone who manages to sneak a peek. Her collection consists of pieces of wood from far off planets, bullet casings from a Kross pistol, a small doll from the village on Vivaldre, and even a skull from an unknown animal. She's protective of her stash of trinkets, since it's highly discouraged to have personal keepsakes in Prol society.

Serge jovially shook his head. "Any plans for adding to your collection on this drop?"

She grabbed Serge's arm casually, "It's a moon! I can't just get out and pick up a rock, I could float away! Or maybe my head would explode first? No, I'd be wearing a helmet!" They both chuckled, "Come on, we should rest up, too much talking will make your throat sore, and we can't have a leader who can't talk!"

"You're right, it's best I take it easy." He slowly sat down at the nearest chair. It creaked under the sudden pressure of a well built soldier.

"WE take it easy you mean." Serge was puzzled at first but eventually took the hint. The door automatically closed behind Kali as she reentered the room and sat next to him. She took a small branch out of her pocket and started carving holes into the center. She glanced at Serge.

"I'll play it for you once we get back." Serge smiled

kindly.

"Just like on Vivaldre."

Victor went to the training pods after the briefing. He climbed into the closest one and booted up a simulation that was the closest he could get to the drop zone he would be landing at. He ran every possible test, varying levels of enemies, allies, ammo, debris, malfunctions, and reinforcements. Every test was ran, and reran until he succeeded without losing any major parts of his ARJAC.

Victor, rest is recommended for both mental and physical health.

"It's okay, I've been put through a lot worse back on Prometheus." He shook his head at the horrors his younger self was forced to do just to survive and booted up another combat simulation.

"One hour until drop time. All personnel involved in the drop to the Mining Facilities are to report to their respective positions." An automated message played throughout the entire ship. Victor rushed to the bays where the Nightcats' ARJACs were held. The halls were a mess of bodies hurrying to their own tasks. Shiphands that were slacking off now scrambled to stations. Steel Soldiers pushed past lower ranking residents on the *Hummingbird* with a sense of authority that is only partly earned. The air was thick with anticipation.

The door opened and the sound of engineers

tweaking parts, barking orders, and ARJAC engines roaring to life washed over Victor. He had changed into his pilot suit, a more fitted version of his uniform with a small breastplate and shoulder port for his A.I. to integrate with the ARJAC. He grabbed his helmet marked with the Nightcat emblem and rushed to his machine.

Victor's helmet had the same color pattern as his uniforms. It was mainly black with a red vertical stripe running down the center. Instead of a visor, like the Iron Corps, Steel Soldier helmets have an opaque surface with three vertical lights across the eyes. The lights' sole purpose is to signal to anyone entering the cockpit of the health of the pilot. Three green lights means the person is healthy, two yellow means they are hurt, and one red blinking light signifies critical condition.

Victor's ARJAC towered over everything that wasn't the other ARJACs. At full height, it stood at about ten meters tall. Missile pods were mounted on each shoulder for long range engagements. Machine guns mounted on the head serve a dual purpose, either to take out infantry or as a last resort when all other weapons have run out of ammo. A knife rested on the left hip for any rare melees that occur. Lastly, the main weapon of Victor's ARJAC, his GR-1s, sat on an enormous weapon rack next to his ARJAC. All Gauss Rifles fire magnetic rounds at breakneck speeds. Since they are usually bulky, both arms are required to fire it with any kind of precision.

"Victor! You're early, even for a newcomer!" An engineer shouted from the scaffolding next to the head of Victor's ARJAC. "I need to run a few tests so hop in here!"

Victor climbed the scaffolding and into the cockpit. The head slid forward, encapsulating Victor inside the torso.

A dim red light lit Victor's controls. His hands were dedicated to control sticks with multiple buttons and a trigger. Each foot had a pedal, the left pedal is to command the ARJAC to jump, while the right pedal is for acceleration. The joysticks help control with fine tuning how an ARJAC functions, as well as the integrated A.I. that the Prol have begun to use. A dashboard of buttons and switches lay spread out in front of Victor.

He flicked a switch on the left part of his seat and a tube unhinged from above. He jammed it into the A.I. port on his shoulder. *Synchronizing with ARJAC designation FS-10G "Nightcat 4."* Victor flicked all the switches on, one by one. *Engine: Online. Sensory Cameras: Online. Joint rotation: Online. Oxygen supply: Full. Radar Pulse: Online.* A low bass filled the cockpit as the radar did a short range pulse. *Helmet integration: awaiting pilot.*

Victor put his helmet on and plugged into his seat with the back of it. Three green lights flicked on after reading his vital signs. Victor could see what the ARJAC sensors were receiving. *Helmet integration: complete. All systems are active, Victor.*

"Thanks Arjie," Victor thanked his A.I.

The engineer stood in front of Victor's ARJAC, waving to get his attention. He cupped his hands around his mouth "Alright Victor since this is your first time in this machine outside of simulations, I need to run some compatibility tests! We'll move the scaffolding so sit tight for a sec! The engineers rolled the creaking scaffolding away from the ARJAC.

"Alright Victor, stand up to your full height!." The machine whirred and hummed as the engine worked until both knees were off the ground, and it was standing at full height, with hands at its sides. "Alright Victor, now pick up that Gauss Rifle right there on the rack!" Victor reached to his right, picked up the rifle off of the rack, and held it in standard combat drop fashion, across the chest, as close as possible. "Alright Victor now brace yourself we're gonna attach the missiles!" Four mechanical fitting arms descended and firmly placed the two round missile pods on the ARJAC's shoulders.

"Okay Victor! Looks like you're good to go! We're gonna clear out all the clutter! Have fun waiting for the drop!" The engineer did a circular motion with his finger and all the help started clearing away the scaffolding and ammunition boxes around Victor. Victor waved slightly and then remained motionless.

He let go of the controls, sitting back in his seat, but he had to keep his helmet on. Every once in a while the ARJAC's head would move slightly as Victor watched people scurry around the bay. He watched the other Nightcats enter, do their systems checks, then remain motionless like him.

When Rutri was done with his systems checks, and was waiting motionless, Victor pointed his head straight at Rutri's ARJAC. He squeezed the trigger for his head-mounted machine guns. *Victor, IFF suggests this is a friendly unit. I have not fired a round because of this. If this is an error you may fire now, but if this is a friendly, any further actions will be considered betrayal to the Prol Intergalactic Alliance.*

Victor chuckled "That would've given him a good spook though wouldn't you agree?"

What felt like hours later, Victor was still waiting in the cockpit. The radio was silent. He felt sleep creeping in.

Victor, this is not the time to be dozing off. "Damn, sorry. I really shouldn't have come this early then. How long until drop?"

Five minutes until drop time.

More silence. Men and women were working with revitalized enthusiasm. Last minute checks were made and orders being barked were drowned out by the sheer volume of mechanical grinding.

One minute until drop.

Suddenly, the radio sparked to life, "Alright Nightcats look alive!" Serge barked. "Everyone knows the proper dropping procedure so just follow that and try not to die!"

Victor adjusted himself in his seat and shook off any tiredness he had. He braced his ARJAC as the drop bay doors swung open.

His legs dangled briefly before the harness let go. Below him was the endless black of space. A quarter of his view was filled with a glowing pale orb. He plummeted towards the moon's surface. To his left Kali's four legged machine was curled up like a dead spider. Serge was to his right, braced in a similar fashion to him, legs slightly bent, shoulder width apart with Gauss Rifle held close. Victor couldn't see Rutri so he must have been behind him somehow.

"Has he already started going towards the facility?" Victor muttered. "While still dropping? That's insane there's asteroids and satellites around he could crash into one and die."

Twenty seconds until landing, Victor. Activating thrusters to prevent damage upon impact. The A.I. then told Victor about standard landing procedures. A pack had been put on all the ARJAC's backs that had two high-power thrusters for landing from high altitudes. They are meant as a one-time use tool. The heat during use becomes too much for the frames, warping or even melting some parts.

The four landed with a cloud of gray-blue dust and four ground shaking thuds. Victor could only feel one other landing, he must have been third to hit the surface. The dust settled painfully slow. The official meeting point, designated operation point alpha, was still a small distance away. Rutri had already made it halfway there.

Victor followed Rutri at top speed. He caught up relatively quickly, with a huge dust cloud coughing up behind him. As he overtook Rutri he gave him a friendly pat on the shoulder. Rutri replied with a single finger.

When the team converged on operation point

alpha, the tone shifted from friendly to military. "Connect to the satellite feed, Nightcats." Serge pointed upward. Everyone's helmets displayed a live video from an orbiting satellite overlooking their target mining facility. "This is our target, once again we'll make our way from the East. There should be airlocks there for us to use. Cat four, scout that out for us, make sure we are still not expected. We'll come in once you give the all clear. We'll meet at operation point bravo."

"Yessir!" Victor cut his satellite feed and rushed to the facility with a whirlwind of moon dust kicking up behind him. He slid down craters big enough to fit a freighter comfortably. He climbed hills as tall as skyscrapers. He didn't see any signs of habitation. Whenever Victor scanned the horizon all he saw was rocks, hills, and craters.

After a ten minute hike in total silence besides the sound of the ARJAC's footsteps reverberating through the machine, his A.I. finally broke his mental silence.

We are approaching the facility now, you should be able to see it on your visual feed.

Victor crested a small hill to overlook a brightly lit, sprawling city. There were not many tall buildings, since there was a dome overhead, locking in the breathable air. Districts were separated by large strips in the ground, emergency airlocks in case the dome became damaged. Most of the time this was because of meteor showers. In the center of the city was the quarry. The city was minuscule in comparison to the massive size of this man-made crater. Cranes and loading walkers, bipedal forklifts used when terrain is not safe for wheeled vehicles, dotted the wall-like road snaking down into the seemingly bottomless pit. Lights speckled the sides of the quarry.

Analysis shows that only 10% of the resources from the quarry constructed the city.

Victor whistled audibly at the sheer size of the rocky complex. "Alright I think we're good to send the others up. Arjie, do you have any hostiles on the sensors?"

The radar pulsed, letting out a low, drawn out tone. *Negative.*

"Okay connect me to the Nightcats." A brief static followed by a quick beep sounded in the helmet. "This is Cat four, I have a visual on the facility. Minimal hostiles, if any."

Serge answered back, "Roger that Cat four, we are moving to your position. Hold there unless something comes up."

"Affirmative. I will continue to scan for hostiles," Victor cut the radio there and waited with as low a profile as his hulking machine would allow him. For another time that felt longer than it was, he was left alone with his thoughts. His A.I. wasn't much of a companion. It was much too formal. It couldn't hold a conversation even if Victor had an instruction manual.

The three arrived with a small cloud of dust trailing them. Kali broke the radio silence, "It's a miracle that the city isn't filled with this dust. There has to be a way for them to clean the air."

"The city has a dome around it. The quarry air never touches the inside." Rutri sharply answered. "We blast the dome, the city dies. Simple."

Kali seemed taken aback by Rutri's simple, yet effective thinking. "Those are civilians, Cat three. We should try to just take the facility without involving killing innocent lives."

Serge cut in, "The briefing says to neutralize the facility. Whatever happens to the city doesn't concern us." He sounded defeated, "Those are the orders."

"Sir, would it be possible to ask the White Camels to do a precision strike on the base? I know they're across the moon but they only have gravity to worry about, no wind here." Victor suggested.

Serge was quiet for a second. "Alright let me see." He was silent again for a minute. "Negative, the gravity and curve of the moon don't line up with the velocity of the matter cannon. We're going in Nightcats."

The three left Kali looking over the facility as overwatch. They slid down the dusty hill into the city. Victor and Serge stopped themselves before hitting the dome protecting the city. Rutri didn't stop. He crashed through the dome. Shattering the glass-like material. The air instantly started rushing out, bringing trash and even a car into the barren land. Victor saw a few bodies thrown into the vacuum too.

Kali was furious. "Rutri what in the name of the Triumvirate are you doing?! You're killing thousands of people by doing this! Why?!"

"Quickest way to the facility. They're part of the Kross rebellion, their lives don't matter to begin with." He said flatly.

The other two followed silently. Rutri walked through buildings and waded through cars and people in a direct path towards the center of the city. Pets fled from their homes, suffocating people were crushed beneath his feet if they were in the way. Some tried to stop him by ramming their vehicles into his feet. He simply kicked them away, sending the car careening into houses and shops.

A few people shot at the three with handguns and other small arms. They were mowed down by the machine guns mounted on the ARJACs' heads. The police tried to set up roadblocks and were met with similar fates. A facility worker tried to wrestle Rutri with her loading walker, but it was a flyweight at best. With no guns or actual hands to grapple with, she stood no chance.

Rutri's ARJAC became covered in blood, dust, and the remains of buildings by the time they reached the other side of the city. He broke down the other side of the dome as well, making the entire section of the city a vacuum.

"Well since we're already here." Serge paused to absorb the destruction he just watched. "Everyone launch your remote explosive into the quarry. Make sure to target your designated areas for maximum facility destruction."

Victor. Be advised: a small quake has just occurred.

Be careful of your footing. Victor braced. *Tremors match standard White Camels B.O.B. main Matter Cannon wave pattern.*

They launched the explosives in a triangular form. Serge aimed North, Victor aimed Southeast, and Rutri aimed Southwest. They all quickly made their way back through the path Rutri carved and up to Kali.

Serge nodded and Kali detonated the explosives. Fire and dust bellowed into the air. Half the city was incinerated because of the hole in the dome. The rest was in chaos from having to set up the special barriers to airlock the city that was still relatively safe.

They all stood in silence watching the smoke billow from the quarry for what seemed like a lifetime. "Cat Lead to Hummingbird, requesting extraction of four units. Mission accomplished. No obvious signs of ARJAC manufacturing facilities. Secondary objective has also been completed." There was a pause. "No signs at the Alpha Facility either? Damn."

Kali turned to Serge, "You never told us about a secondary objective!"

Serge paused, "Our secondary objective was to damage the city beyond repair. The higher ups thought it was better than cutting off supply lines. Nip it in the bud or something." He let out an audible sigh, "The rest of the city will most likely turn to anarchy or starve before they can rebuild."

Victor couldn't look away from the destruction. "Shit."

2

Weeks passed with very little mention of the massacre on Jenrika. After a few days of silence around the table and in the rooms, the team slowly returned to what they considered to be normal day-to-day life. Training occurred at the usual times, standard briefings were quick, and the food was average. An emergency message came through to the *Hummingbird* stating that the Prol forces on Nazar-D were heavily outnumbered and in need of immediate backup. They had their new orders.

Victor sat in his ARJAC going over the plan for his second drop, but his first real battle. He was dropping with the Nightcats right into the middle of the Kross lines to draw fire while the main forces pushed through and met up with them for the final assault on the main Kross base of Nazar-D. If they dropped in the correct spot, they should be in some resemblance of cover. It was likely no casualties would be taken.

Nazar-D has the driest climate in Kross controlled space. Only the poles have water, but very little at that. The hottest parts of the planet could boil ice the second it came in contact with the atmosphere during the summers. Despite all that, the planet is a strategic location for shipping routes and communications. A massive trading hub orbited the planet. Its docking ports were almost always busy before the Kross Rebellion. Now the docks are used as staging grounds for attacks to neighboring systems.

"Hey Serge?" Victor broke the silence as the four ARJACs dangled over the closed doors below their feet. "There's no catch to this mission right? It's just a regular combat drop?"

"Yeah, just get in and shoot anything that doesn't register friendly to the IFF tags," his voice was monotone and gruff.

We are dropping in thirty seconds Victor, be ready. The talking stopped as everyone's A.I. told them the same thing at the same time.

The four shifted slightly as they plummeted towards the surface of Nazar-D. There were no asteroids or satellites orbiting the planet, so the Nightcats could more freely control their drop to maximize landing accuracy. As they got closer to the surface, FLAK cannons attempted to shoot them out of the sky. The airbursting shells jostled the ARJACs as they careened towards the wasteland. Victor could hear the shrapnel peppering his hull. His head knocked against the back of his seat and his vision temporarily went to gray and white specks. Most shots missed the ARJACs but one managed to graze Rutri. He spun wildly with sparks and smoke billowing from his back but managed to regain control. His landing pack appeared to be damaged.

"Cat three, are you ok?" Serge asked. "Your thrusters look damaged."

"It's not like I can do anything else but try to land, Sir." Rutri's voice was a calm anger. He had not liked getting shot before he could fight back.

The other three landed in a cloud of sand, exhaust fumes, and the dust of any infantry unfortunate enough to be directly under them. Rutri landed with a sharp *thud*. He created a crater filled with soldiers torn in two, or many more pieces. They were launched into the air by the shock wave of the gargantuan metal machine landing at near terminal velocity. Dead soldiers lay half buried in the sand, their faces a calm nervousness. They hadn't had time to acknowledge they were dead.

"We landed in an area with minimal heavy vehicles, neutralize everything then regroup at Cat three, he seems to be a little stuck." Serge chuckled as small arms fire ricocheted off of his armor. Rutri's legs were buried in sand up to his waist. He was violently swinging his arms to kill anything he could reach. His head mounted machine guns roared a storm of bullets every time he looked in a different direction.

Victor began fighting the second his A.I. said it was safe to move. He deftly jumped over tanks as he put a single Gauss Rifle slug into the top, penetrating all the way through into the sand below. He made sure to step on any anti-vehicle infantry trying to target his squad mates without them knowing. Victor passed by Serge as he was dueling the only enemy ARJAC in the area.

Serge feinted with his knife as he drilled a hole into the ARJACs' left shoulder with his head mounted machine guns. The Kross ARJAC stumbled as its right knee was punctured by Serge's knife. He drove the knife home in the ARJAC's head. He finished off the ARJAC with a single shot straight through the cockpit.

Victor, enemy reinforcements are approaching from the front line. Heavy armor is to be expected.

Victor and Serge made their way to Rutri to dig him out of the sand. He was already furiously clawing to try to dig himself out. Kali had found the highest point for her to provide support, which happened to be a landing platform on top of a particularly tall sand dune. She spotted the incoming reinforcements before the others. While they finished digging Rutri out, she shot a heavy Gauss slug over Rutri's head. It cracked past Serge's and Victor's heads and pierced an enemy ARJAC. It fell into the sand after losing the entirety of its torso.

"Next time tell us when you're shooting so close! Nearly took all our heads off!" Victor was shocked at how close Kali had shot between them.

Serge laughed "You'll get used to it! She knows how we move and she definitely has the skill to make shots like that perfectly." Kali gave them a thumbs up.

"Looks like the reinforcements are here!" Kali was already lining up her next shot.

Rutri managed to pull himself out of the sand only to find his legs were slightly damaged, his knee joints were practically shattered along with his left ankle. He could barely stand. Rutri let out a low groan of frustration and fired a barrage of missiles into the oncoming wave of angry Kross. They emerged from the swirling sands one by one, opening fire on the closest target, Rutri.

Rounds bounced off of his armor, some penetrating past the thick plating, damaging internal components. Every piercing shot knocked him back as bits and pieces of his ARJAC chipped off like a pickax against brittle stone. A tank shell took off his entire arm, flinging his heavy Gauss Rifle into the sand along with some of his torso.

He tried to charge into the fight, but his legs were still filled with sand and damaged from the hard landing. He limped forward, firing any weapon he had left as he was slowly disassembled by force. He managed to kill one or two of the tanks, but was rendered useless within seconds.

Rutri's ARJAC was barely more than a smoking pile of rubble. Most of his front armor plating was gone. His legs were little more than twisted skeletons of what they once were. He was missing his right arm and most of his left.

"Cat four! We're going back to Cat two's position. There's no way we can take them head on!" Serge barked his orders into the radio.

The three stood their ground and used the height to their advantage. They took out any advancing Kross out of cover as a team. Most shots hit the sand below the Nightcats   with a thud. In moments the sand was littered with ARJACs and tanks billowing smoke. Craters and footprints were scattered among the dunes.

"Were there supposed to be this many hostiles,

sir?" Victor was running out of ammunition fast, and everything was overheating as more and more sand flew into the exhaust and heat sinks. His uniform was drenched in sweat. The cockpits were fully enclosed and air tight, but it was not standard to have air conditioning and the outside heat had started to creep in.

A lone Kross ARJAC managed to crest the hill they were hiding behind. Serge glanced in its direction before tackling it to the ground, his right arm still aiming over the dune, firing blindly. With his left arm, Serge pinned the Kross ARJAC to the sand. With his head mounted machine guns, Serge fired point blank into the torso, slowly punching a hole into the cockpit. The ARJAC struggled as best it could in the consuming sand before it quickly went limp, his machine guns finally shredding the pilot.

A single shot ripped through Victor's head, leaving him without any visuals. Quickly, Victor climbed down what he thought was the safer side of the dune. "Cat lead, I lost my head, I can't fight anymore."

"You still have some fight in you," Serge replied. "Cat two, can you give me the coordinates of the highest density of Kross?"

"Affirmative," Kali quickly answered. "They are two hundred meters at about ten degrees to the left of Cat four."

"Launch all your missiles into that area!" Serge was confident in Kali's abilities. That's why they survived as long as they had in the war.

"Roger that, launching!" Victor shot a full salvo of missiles. They streaked across the orange tinted sky with a roar. The Kross didn't have time to evade the maelstrom of devastation that hit them all at once. Tanks were destroyed beyond repair, ARJACs were all critically damaged, and if there were any infantry left on the battlefield, they no longer existed. A blackened crater smoked and shimmered, the sand turning into a glossy pit from the sheer heat of the concentrated explosion.

"Alright Victor, you did great," Serge sounded relieved. "As your commanding officer I order you to punch out. There's nothing more you can do from here on out. We'll find a way to make it out alive."

Kali seemed rather calm as well, "We'll all meet up soon, and Cat three, if you can hear me we'll send a rescue team as soon as it's safe!"

Victor lifted his sweat covered helmet's opaque metal visor to see the emergency controls. He opened up a clear plastic cover and punched the eject button.

Victor, please confirm that you are ejecting from the ARJAC.

"This is Nightcat four, punching out!"

"See you soon kid," Serge muttered.

Confirmed. Ejecting cockpit from main unit. Activating internal life support. Emergency homing beacon activated.

Launching.

The cockpit tore through the ARJAC and blasted into space at speeds barely safe for humans. Victor put on the oxygen mask connected to the life support system and closed the visor again to monitor the amount of fuel and oxygen he had left. There was also the possibility of friendlies on the short range radar. He didn't want to think about hostiles on his radar.

"Well now it looks like we wait." He crossed his arms and closed his eyes. "Let me know if there's anything serious, Arjie."

Confirmed.

A few hours later, Victor opened his eyes. "So was it just me or was there a lot more Kross than the battle projection originally said?"

Battle projections stated there would be a medium sized and heavily fatigued reinforcement wave.

"And what did we encounter?"

Analysis shows the Nightcats encountered a fresh reinforcement army of large or greater size.

"That's what it looked like too," he sighed. "So what's the plan until help arrives?"

Recommended course of action is hyperstasis.

A bolt of panic shot through his body, "Why? What's going on? Hyperstasis is only used during times of extreme circumstances of survival."

Scans show there are no friendly IFF tags in the

range of the distress beacon. His A.I. paused briefly. *There are no friendlies anywhere within visual range either. The Hummingbird has left the planet.*

Victor slumped into the seat and went limp. "Looks like hyperstasis is the way to go then," he said flatly. "Arjie, initiate hyperstasis procedure."

Please confirm.

"Hyperstatis confirmed."

Confirmed. Initiating. Restricting oxygen flow. Shutting down cockpit lights. Setting the homing beacon to pulse. Cutting feed from helmet optics. Checking for faults. Zero faults detected. Injecting hyperstasis compound.

Victor instantly felt extremely tired. His muscles barely worked. His eyes couldn't stay open no matter how hard he tried. Before his consciousness left him, he thought he heard the A.I. say one more thing.

Projected time of sleep is ten years. Chance of survival: five percent.

3

Victor sat alone at his usual table in the mess hall. Soldiers all around him talked about something he couldn't quite understand. Was it about him? The war? Today's food? There was no way to tell. He couldn't seem to bring himself to stand up and ask. The smell of delicious food wafted over to his table, but he still couldn't stand up to get some. *What is going on?* The mess hall looked cleaner than usual. There weren't any bits of food on the floor that had fallen from a tray. There were no cleaning robots lazily rolling under the tables. The chefs were unrecognizable. *Are they new? What happened to the old chefs? Why can't I make out their faces?* Serge and the rest walked up to the chefs and asked for their usual meals. They sat with Victor and spoke to each other, as if he wasn't there.

One year has passed. Administering recommended amounts of nutrients. Condition stable.

He stood surrounded by unfamiliar ARJACs in a drop bay. Engineers worked tirelessly on each one of them, a lone drone of voices and sparks of machinery filled the air. There was no way of telling what they were saying. ARJACs of all sizes and shapes stood motionless. Some had weapons Victor had only read about in training. Standard Gauss Rifles, matter canons, and machine guns littered the weapon racks scattered throughout the bay. There were also massive melee weapons. *Is this some kind of gladiator arena?* Hammers, axes, swords, and even ARJAC arms shaped into spears rested in between the firearms. An alarm sounded, then above two of the ARJACs the drop lights started flashing. The hatches opened and they plummeted to an unknown planet.

Two years have passed. Administering recommended amounts of nutrients. Conditions are dropping slightly. Administering recommended amount of Compound B.

Victor stood in a field of flowers. Rolling hills led to far away snow covered mountain peaks. He turned and looked in every direction, but he was all alone. Nothing but flowers, bees, butterflies, and other insects were around. The wind caressed his face gently. He did not smell anything. Victor had only seen flowers in textbooks and pictures. Petals leapt from their planted positions and swirled into the blue sky dotted with small, puffy clouds. A spontaneous gust of wind knocked him on his back. Victor didn't bother to stand up, he just stared into the sky, watching the clouds roll into the horizon. The flowers around his head gave the sky a frame of red, yellow, pink, purple, and blue.

Three years have passed. Administering five percent higher than recommended amount of nutrients. Condition has stabilized. Monitoring for any changes.

Victor sat in his cockpit. He looked at all the flashing and pulsing lights. It was dimly lit solely because of the buttons and small information screens. Food was scattered on the floor. He was taken aback at first, but quickly accepted the existence of the floor food, and picked up the nearest burger. He unwrapped the paper and took a big bite. It tasted like metal and dust. He quickly jerked the burger back to see it was made out of screws, bolts, and various metal scraps. He picked up a drink and tried to wash out the metallic taste. He gulped in a mouthful of oil, and spat it out faster than he thought was possible. He threw the drink against the floor and a thick black liquid oozed out. Victor searched for his helmet to put on. He didn't want to look at all of this amazing food, not being able to eat anything. He couldn't find it anywhere.

Four years have passed. Administering new recommended amounts of nutrients. Condition dropping. Administering recommended amount of Compound T. Administering recommended amount of Compound H.

Victor was back in a cockpit, but it wasn't *his* cockpit. There was no helmet to see what the ARJAC saw. There was a cylindrical shape to the cockpit, with many odd shaped windows to directly see the enemy. A primitive reticle shown in the center of a small transparent monitor. Buttons and dials littered the desk-like semicircle around the seat. Screens showed the state of the strange ARJAC, any damaged parts, and ammo counters for some of the weapons. *Why are there lasers? What kind of ARJAC carries weaponized lasers?* The control sticks were a primitive looking airplane style of controls, with only one stick and an accelerator for the left hand. There were still foot pedals but Victor refrained from touching them, since he was unsure what kind of ARJAC this even was, or if it was something else. *Is this some sort of ancient relic?* The ARJAC powered on, stood up on its own, and started sprinting at the closed doors ahead of it.

Five years have passed. Condition continuing to drop. All compounds are empty. Administering the last amount of nutrients stored.

Victor stood in a bathroom. It looked similar to the ones on the *Hummingbird.* Nobody else was in the bathroom with him, which was strange because of how massive it was. Stalls stretched so far the walls and floors curved with the ship. *Have I gone to the bathroom yet or have I just walked in here? Where is everyone else?* Victor listened for anyone talking or footsteps or SOMETHING but it was dead silent. He turned on the faucet to wash his hands, after a second he realized it was not water that was coming out. It was a thick red liquid with a horrible stench. He tripped backwards onto the floor. All the faucets started to pour the same liquid. The liquids filled up the sinks, and started to overflow onto the tiled floor.

Six years have passed. Conditions are dropping steadily. Survival chances are dropping. Victor, good luck.

Black. Victor floated in a completely black space. No stars, no lights, no wind. He looked around for anything to get his bearings. You stared straight up and saw something. Was it a pinhole of light? Was it a star? Something brushed past his leg and caressed his calves. It gripped him so tight he screamed. But nothing came out. He felt a rush as he was pulled downward, into darker and darker black.

Seven years have passed. Condition failing. Survival is

still guaranteed upon awakening. Serious medical attention is not necessary yet.

Victor faced a man at a desk. They sat face to face in a large, open cave. The man shuffled his papers and fixed his glasses. He looked up at Victor and smiled. He walked back to a stalagmite and reached behind it. He pulled out some paperwork and threw it lazily onto his desk. He slumped back down and started reading it over. He shook his head in confusion.

Eight years have passed. Entering advanced power saving mode. Victor, I shall check in yearly, so hang in there.

Nine years have passed. Condition critical. Minor medical attention is needed upon recovery. Scans show a planet is nearby. Stay alive Victor.

Ten years have passed. Please. Hang in there.

4

Victor blinked awake, his head drowsy. He couldn't quite get a grip on his thoughts. The training videos about hyperstasis mentioned splitting headaches and nausea, but he felt perfectly fine. "What happened to me?"

Well for starters you're alive, so that's good. But there is a downside to all this.

"What are you talking about Arjie, I feel great! Also have you changed?"

Yes, I seem to have developed a personality of sorts. I think this is because of constant adaptation to you well over the calculated lifespan of a Steel Soldier. Unlike you, I stayed awake the whole time, monitoring your dreams and brain waves.

"Why didn't they tell me this at first?" Victor asked. The training videos were nothing like the real thing.

Nobody lasts this long. Usually.

Victor put his feet on the floor to stand up from the bed he was in. The tiles on the floor weren't cold. "Wait, where the hell am I? This isn't a Prol medbay."

A door slid open and a grease covered woman

walked into Victor's room. "Look at you, looks like you're adjusting well."

"Where am I?" Victor questioned, "Who the hell are you? What do you mean adjusting? I just woke up. Arjie, how long was I asleep for?"

I stopped monitoring after ten, ask her what year it is.

The woman looked confused, "What did you just call me?"

"I have an A.I. implant, I was talking to him, I call him Arjie," Victor explained as he tapped his shoulder.

A metallic sound resonated in the empty room. Victor looked down from where it came from. He saw himself for the first time. He was completely naked. Or at least he had no clothes on. His arms, legs, and body were made of some unknown metal, shining with a dull sheen in the well lit room. Wires and artificial muscle ran through his entire body.

He felt like himself physically, but Victor was not himself at all. He shook his head, trying to rid himself of what he thought was a hallucination. The metal body stayed no matter how much he concentrated on reality.

"What did you do to me?" He shouted.

"I saved your life. Your heart had stopped when I found you. I'm surprised I could copy your brainwaves, they were almost non-existent. The name's Stasha by the way. You're welcome." She held up a small mirror to Victor. It was a plain mirror, with very little extra details.

All function with none of the ornate details of a more expensive mirror. It worked just as well as any other mirror though.

His face was all metallic too, just like his body. He had armor plating around his forehead down to his cheeks. His eyes were nothing but glass slits.

"What happened? What year is it?" Victor asked as he continued to stare disbelieving into his reflection.

"When I found you, it was the twentieth year of the rebellion. Now it's the thirty second," Stasha said flatly.

"I went into hyperstasis in the seventh year." Victor put his head in his hands. "How am I alive?"

"I copied your brain waves and built this body for you. Not too sure how your A.I. friend managed to tag along though." She circled Victor, inspecting her work.

I may have melded with your consciousness while monitoring your vitals. It's just a theory though.

"I'm just happy I still have a life." Victor stood up fully. "I've been told prosthetics take a while to get used to but I've never heard of a full consciousness transfer. How am I able to walk and talk this early?"

"I used your corpse as a reference guide." Stasha shuddered at the memory. "There was nothing else to do with it once I transferred the important stuff over to the computer."

She's talking about your consciousness. I just completed a full scan and found minimal signs of any organic matter.

"So where is it? Or-" he paused. "Where am I?"

"I didn't know what to do with it. If I buried it, it would seem like you're dead, so it's just hanging out in the pod I found you in." She seemed at a loss. It was hard for her to get the wording right.

"Stasha, you have a good reason to be confused, this is the first time someone has had a full consciousness transfer. Or maybe this is a copy?" Victor wasn't sure if he was truly himself anymore. This shell he was in was more than just a human body, it was immortal. Humans have been trying to obtain immortality for centuries, since the dawn of time, so why did he feel so empty?

Hey Victor, I bet you're thinking about wanting to see yourself aren't you? I'm kinda curious too.

The image of what Victor could look like came up in his mind. "Stasha, is it possible to see myself, it, whatever?" He stumbled on his words, sounding less like the machine that he was.

"It's not a pretty sight, but if you want to I guess it's technically your property." Stasha prepared herself to see the shriveled body once again.

Victor staggered at first, but after a few steps with help from Stasha he was walking like he always had been. They made their way down a narrow staircase into an open area. ARJACs lined the walls. Each had their own unique paint schemes. One was red and black, with skulls littering the armor. Another was solid white, while one in the corner was bright blue with the words "STEALTH THIS BITCH" written over the chest.

"So are these all yours?" Victor was amazed at how vibrant each ARJAC was.

"No I just work on them, they belong to the local pirates," She replied with clear disgust in her voice.

Looks like someone has a grudge against the neighborhood ruffians.

They entered a door on the side of the storage bay and descended further. Victor shuddered. He didn't know if it was the cold or his nerves about seeing himself dead. "Can I even feel the temperature?" he muttered.

"You should be able to," Stasha had overheard him. "Your body has environmental sensors. Your little friend must be simulating your feelings for you."

Stasha opened one final door and in a dimly lit basement room, the crashed pod awaited. The paint was chipped off years ago, leaving the bare metal exposed and rusting. The hatch was closed. She turned to Victor, "Last chance to say you don't want to see your own corpse."

Actually I'm curious to see the effects of prolonged hyperstasis.

"I came this far, didn't I?" Victor hesitated and took what he thought was a deep breath. "Open it up."

Stasha pulled a lever by a control panel and the hatch slowly lifted. "Don't bodies usually smell awful?"

"Well that's because you can't smell. Also it's so far gone that everything is either dried up or evaporated." Stasha wrinkled her nose. "It wasn't pleasant when I first found you though."

The hatch lifted enough to reveal the body. It was practically nothing more than a skeleton with skin. The uniform was still in pristine condition. The rest of the pod was a mess of wires, dried refuse, and broken electronics.

Victor, you probably don't want to hear this but I'm picking up a signal almost equal to my own. That must mean that somehow, you're technically still alive. However, at this point I can safely say there's no point of return.

"You must be joking," Victor stared in disbelief, hardly able to keep himself upright. Stasha stared at him wide-eyed and very confused.

"Did I miss something?"

"Arjie says I'm technically still alive. Or at least a version of himself is." He nodded towards the pod.

"Your vital signs flatlined months ago how can you be so sure? The most recent scans came up negative again and again."

I can overclock the artificial brain unit with very little detriment to you.

"He says he overclocked my brain," Victor flatly said.

"Wow," she paused in thought. "Are you sure that's

not dangerous?"

"Arjie thinks it's safe."

"Well I guess I'll have to trust your A.I. friend. So anyway, what do you want to do with yourself?" Stasha put her hand on her hip and raised her brow.

"Well I guess this is technically the new me, so the old me should be tossed aside. Right?" He didn't feel right saying that.

"Hey it's your body don't look at me." Stasha inspected the pod once more. She looked at it with a grave familiarity.

Victor walked over and touched the skin he once was in. A long silence made the room feel like a midnight graveyard. Victor gave his body a pat on the shoulder, and the arm fell to the floor with a crunchy thud.

They both shuddered and Victor nodded to Stasha to close the pod again. "We'll give him. Me. A proper burial. Can we use any of those ARJACs to dig a grave or do we have to do it the old fashioned way?"

"I do have a construction model you can use. I'm assuming you don't need my help on this one Mr. Prol Soldier?"

"Yeah, I can manage. Also how did you know all that?"

"Well for starters the patch on your chest was a dead giveaway. As for the Steel Soldier part, well the escape pod isn't the standard EP-1 that all interstellar ships carry. Upon further inspection I found out that your fancy escape pod also had complex control modules. It's extremely similar to the ARJAC controls the pirates use."

Victor was speechless.

This girl knows her stuff.

The pod was hauled back to the surface and placed in a hole big enough to fit the bulbous vessel. There were no other buildings, just trees and grass. Birds chirped nervously at the commotion below the canopy. Victor lowered the pod down, and before covering it with dirt, he saluted, and severed the pod in half.

"Sorry about the slow death, twenty five years is a hell of a long time." Victor covered it all with dirt.

Do you want me to simulate the tears you should be weeping?

"No, please don't."

He walked back towards the giant workshop. Stasha was waiting, leaning up against the massive metal door. "So what do you plan on doing now? I have a communication relay if you want to contact your friends. That might not be the wisest idea though."

"Why's that?" He asked.

"Well," she paused for effect. We are at the heart of the rebellion."

"You don't mean–" Victor knew the answer before

she said it.

"Yup, we're on Earth. Homeworld of Penelope Kross, leader of the Kross Rebellion," Stasha said with pride.

Victor was stunned. Earth was across all of Kross controlled space from Nazar-D. "Well I suppose my life as a Prol soldier is over. They won't find me all the way out here."

"That was his life, not yours," She motioned to the burial site. Stasha was genuinely curious how a young abandoned soldier would act. "But what are you going to *do*?"

5

Today something crashed into the woods nearby. It happened at roughly 7 p.m. so I'll have to check it out tomorrow in more detail.

It seems to be some sort of launched object. Judging by the engravings on the hull, it appears to be made by the Prol. "Triumvirate Manufacturing" is a dead giveaway. I'll try to pry it open over the weekend. Chubb's ARJAC still needs repairs, and she doesn't like to wait.

I rushed the job on Chubb's ARJAC, it's not like they have any eye for details. The pod has piqued my curiosity. What's a Prol pod doing all the way out here? If it was a bomb it would've detonated by now. Lost resources?

It's an escape pod! I pried it open and a shriveled up dead guy was inside. Just how long has he been in there? It looks like a multipurpose cockpit so maybe I can scrap it if anything is still working.

Scans showed some kind of activity from the guy! HOW IS HE STILL ALIVE!? This just gets weirder and weirder. Guess I have no choice but to save his shriveled ass from true death. How am I going to do this though? Hang in there.

Chubb sent her machine back to me again. It looks like

she thinks it took a critical hit during a raid. I'll take the luck that was given to me and repair it normally from now on. I can't be following in my parents' footsteps.

Chubb's ARJAC was repaired on time and scans show my dead friend is still alive. So how am I going to save him exactly? I'll have to make a scanner that saves and transfers data.

After a few weeks, the prototype of the "Brain Transfer 1" has been made. It works similar to some sort of short range radar. I dragged the pod into the storage basement, I can't have anyone seeing this Prol pod on my property.

The guy's head has been scanned, and transferred into a central computer that can hold his (data?) until I figure out how to make him a new body, cuz there's no way his old one is going to make it.

Drafts for a head have been made, if you're gonna have a new body it should look cool right? Comic book style or maybe those old sci fi movies.

I transferred the data into the head and nothing happened. Is he actually just dead and the system is picking up background noise?

The "Brain Transfer 2" has been built. Let's hope this one works. I don't want this to be a huge waste of time.

Same scan as last time (what the hell is keeping him alive?) Data looks the same at a close inspection. (Am I even racing against time here?) I can't give it a full comparison to the first one. I've wiped the head of all data.

The head seems to be functioning! There's no speech but analysis shows it has some sort of primitive thinking. These are good steps. Hang in there.

There doesn't seem to be much else I can think of to change. (Is this the end for my friend here?) I'll try developing a third iteration of the "Brain Transfer" and DOUBLE CHECK all the data.

Third time I scanned this shriveled mess. Data seems roughly the same as the first two.

The problem was that the scanner was picking up the mechanisms of the pod as well as his brain! It'll be extremely risky, but I'll have to temporarily remove the body from the pod keeping him "alive."

It appears that he's pumped full of something. The tubes and needles have long dried up but his body still has been altered. I can shut off the pod completely with little change to him.

Data transfer #3 success! The data lines aren't nearly as long this time so this could be it.

Cross referencing the other two iterations of pod man's brain scan, there are definitely similarities.

He's MOVING! He spoke to me today and found out all sorts of things about him. He's technically older than I am, but about half his life was spent in hyperstasis. How did he last that long?

Victor and Stasha sat in a dingy kitchen, the drone of the overhead lights and Stasha occasionally eating her food were the only sounds. It looked appetizing enough for the limited resources she had. Victor sat across from her, staring intently at her food. He picked up a fork and knife and looked down at his empty plate. A familiar meal phased into existence in front of him. Sausage, toast, and waffle fries.

"I'm still not used to the whole *hallucinogenic food thing.*" Victor stabbed a sausage and put it into his nonexistent mouth. The sausage snapped and warm, delicious juices rushed to cover the surface area of his mouth. He chewed with his nonexistent teeth until he was able to swallow.

"And I'm still not used to you eating air like it was a full course meal." Stasha shook her head and watched as he picked up the toast carefully, making sure no crumbs got into his lap.

"Hey you remember what Arjie said, if I don't eat I'll go insane or something."

These are the facts. Don't look at me, I'm just the one in your head. You're lucky I only make you go to the bathroom when it's convenient for you.

"Are you sure this is really necessary though? It's weirding me out just watching this." Stasha shuddered as she stood up to get another cup of coffee. Victor followed her to the sink and started to rinse his plate. "Victor, that's just a clean plate. You're wasting water."

"Oh," he paused. "Right," he paused again. "So what are you doing today, I think I've finally mastered this new body."

"Well, if you MUST help, today I have to finish the repairs on Chubb's ARJAC and then get started on the repairs and modifications of Polpy's. Also," she grabbed Victor's "leftovers" and threw them at him. He flinched and wiped his face, "you clearly haven't mastered it." She laughed as she walked through the doors into the ARJAC bay.

Well that was just rude. Why do you put up with her so much? She's not too different from Kali in that aspect.

Victor shrugged and followed Stasha. He snatched an old, patched jacket from the hook before catching up.

"So the blue one is Chubb's?"

"Yeah she really isn't known for her... *quiet side.*"

The ARJAC had been painted with more profanities since Victor saw it the first time. The Welterweight ARJAC had taken a beating, with holes littering the torso and legs, most likely from infantry with anti-armor capabilities.

"She's gonna have a field day repainting this thing." Stasha said as she glossed her hand over the ARJAC. "Victor, you can be on crane duty. Lift 'er up!" He pulled the lever to lift up the ARJAC enough to lessen the load on the legs. Stasha sawed off squares of armor plating that had fused with the structure of the ARJAC. "I wish they let me use better armor plating. This faux steel that they use is terrible." Stasha lifted her welding goggles and signaled for the ARJAC to be lifted slightly higher.

The two spent most of the day in silence, working

on repairing Chubb's ARJAC, using only simple hand gestures to communicate what to do. A few hours before work was over, they had finished work on Chubb's ARJAC, and could move onto working on Polpy's.

"So what kind of upgrades are we giving this blindingly white hunk of junk?" Victor maneuvered the crane into position above the ARJAC.

"We're replacing the legs," Stasha sounded excited.

"This thing's not even a Bantamweight, it shouldn't need better legs than what it already has, right?" Victor pulled the lever to lift the ARJAC fully off the ground.

"Not an upgrade, more like a-" Stasha paused and thought. "A change." She nodded her head at the corner of the bay housing Polpy's ARJAC. Six legs sprawled out in all directions.

Victor reeled back, "We're making this thing into a spider? That is not something I would want to see coming at me."

"You think that might be the point?" Stasha retorted. She started dismantling the waist of the ARJAC, placing the parts into a nearby bin with a light toss. The old metal bits clinked off of each other and settled in a messy pile.

The sun was setting as the old legs finally came off of the ARJAC, a loud metallic bang resonated throughout the workshop.

Are we done yet? I'm bored as hell.

Stasha signaled to lock the crane and shut it down.

"So Stasha, what are we going to do with the old legs?" Victor asked.

"Well, the Demolition Proxy didn't say what to do with them." She lightly held her chin, deep in thought.

"You think we can use it to make an ARJAC for me? I'm dying to pilot one again."

Good one.

"Hmmmm," Stasha looked over at the bipedal legs.

"I specialized in lighter weighted ARJAC's back in the day, I can even tune it to my liking."

"Victor, you don't know how to repair an ARJAC, let alone build one."

"Well yeah, that's where you come in. Do you really want to work for pirates the rest of your life? Aren't they ruthless killers wanted by both the Kross and Prol?"

"You don't even know the start of how badly I want them gone."

Victor ate his nonexistent food while Stasha drank some coffee and looked over the floor plans for the pirates' base. She circled some areas, connected others with lines, and labeled just about everything until the map was practically written all over with some form of ink. She mumbled to herself, going over the plans in her head one last time, making small adjustments where she thought they were needed.

She nodded to herself and put her pen down, finished her coffee in one gulp, and sighed. "Alright Victor stop eating air, we have a base to infiltrate. The meeting starts now."

Victor quickly put his clean dishes away and sat back down at the table. The act of putting "used" dishes away was still a mental hurdle for Victor, but he was less hesitant to do it now. They clinked against other plates and mugs. "Let's hear it."

Stasha quickly looked over the map one more time. "Alright, you have to remember all this because we can't communicate once you ship out. They check all their imports with great detail, so I'm telling them I'm sending over a repair android so that they don't have to send their ARJACs to me for basic repairs. You do know how to repair an ARJAC right?"

"Arjie will tell me what to do. He's seen you work," he said flatly and with confidence.

"Okay, that's relatively good to hear. Anyway, once they get used to you, I'll leave it up to you to determine when that might be, start by cutting off the life support when they are all sleeping. The main power switch will be located here." She pointed to a section of the map circled in red. "It's a standard LS-5471 so it should be relatively easy to understand. Remember to do this at the beginning of the night, since it'll take a while to actually start to be lethal. You'll be fine, since you essentially run on a self charging battery. That's option one." She paused and took a breath.

"Sounds easy enough, but this plan takes a while. I didn't go to acting school so there's that risk," Victor felt at home. He remembered what it was like to be in the Nightcats.

"Right. That's why we have plan B."

Victor stroked his chin. "Let's hear it."

"Plan B is that." She pointed out a window to the ARJAC deck. "We smuggle you into one of those and you just start blasting when they least expect it." It sounded like she preferred this plan.

"Sounds dangerous. How many ARJACs do they have in total?" Victor was swept into the routine of briefing before a mission.

"Let's see, there's Polpy's Spider, Chubb's Bruiser, you know those. There's four more that aren't here right now. Two spares, and two unique ones. There's Grisly's ARJAC, which is a nippy little machine, suits her well. Also Coxswain, who has a command network set up all within the head of his ARJAC. It has satellite hacking capabilities and so much more."

Victor leaned back in his chair, "These guys sure are high tech for a band of misfit pirates."

"They have a good mechanic." Stasha bragged unenthusiastically.

"Do we have a plan C?"

"I'm a mechanic not a war general, Victor. You should have come up with these plans."

Victor closed his eyes and thought for a few seconds.

I have a plan, would you like to hear it?

"Later, Arjie. How about this for a plan? We mix plans A and B! You give me to them as a repair android and I can tamper with their ARJACs while they think I'm just repairing parts. Once I gain their trust, I shut off the life support and blast the place off the map."

That was my plan.

"Where is the base anyway?" Victor couldn't remember if she had ever mentioned it.

"The moon."

"Wasn't that ordered a quarantined zone after a battle there in the second year of the war?"

"That's why it's a perfect spot for a hidden pirate base," she retorted.

Victor nodded, he was impressed they could navigate the tightly packed asteroid field. "Fair enough."

"They'll be here in an hour Victor. You better start practicing your android impression." Stasha made the final preparations for the shipment to the pirates. She held a worn down clipboard and checked off the items as she walked down the rows of boxes and crates. They contained food, general pleasantries, and some hygiene essentials.

Victor paced, still trying to make up his mind as to which plan to do, or which plan to favor when combining the plans. "If I don't act robotic enough they'll suspect something right away, even though fully inorganic consciousness hasn't been developed enough for use. If I smuggle myself into the base in an ARJAC, I could get killed in a one sided firefight. I don't want to try my luck with fighting four on one."

You'll be fine, you're a Steel Soldier. You have every skill necessary to complete a mission like this.

"Yeah, but I've never done one *alone.*" Victor took a look at the white spider-like ARJAC. He shuddered. "I wish I'll never see that again after today. Kali had an ARJAC similar to this one but damn those legs just creep me out."

Victor shook his head and continued pacing. "Wait!" He turned to Stasha, "How am I going to get back here?"

Stasha stopped checking her list and looked up. "Oh, you know, you're right. Can you pilot a spacecraft?"

"Never tried before. I'm very much a one trick pony."

Stasha tapped the pen on her cheek. "My knowledge is pretty basic, I've done it a couple times before. How about this? I'll forget to give them something and in a week's time make the 'delivery.' That way if for whatever reason nothing has happened yet, I'll be safe. That is of course, if I can make it through the asteroids." She paused and looked Victor over. "Oh, and you'll have to go in naked. I know you like wearing my cool jacket but an android with clothes on sparks suspicion."

Victor took off the worn down leather jacket and placed it on a nearby crate. He hung his head and patted the jacket.

Maybe the Demolition Proxy will give you a new look. Let's hope they have some good sense of style.

The radio crackled to life. A gruff woman's voice came on "Hey engineer! We're right above you! Open up!"

Stasha groaned as she pulled the lever to open up the ARJAC bay roof. It creaked as it slowly opened, letting in the piercing sun. An old dropship roared as it slowly entered the building. Anything that wasn't heavy flew to the corners of the bay. Stasha braced herself against a crate and Victor stood as still as he could. The roar became deafening, shutting out the creaking metal walls as the ship descended.

The ship turned off and the deafening roar turned into deafening stillness. The doors opened to reveal a short, portly woman and a very large, muscular man. The woman strutted over to Stasha and snatched the clipboard. She quickly looked over everything and then stared at Victor.

"Who's that?" she said aggressively.

"That's." Stasha paused, trying to think of a name.

"Hello! I am Arjie, I was made by Stasha to assist

you in on site repairs for your ARJACs."

You can't steal my identity like that!

"Too bad," Victor whispered. "For a small monthly fee, I can help with basic repairs and tune-ups. Making it more cost effective for you, and more time effective for everyone! And who might you be?"

Stasha nodded in approval. The woman stared at him for a few seconds.

"I'm Chubb. We're gonna work you to the bone."

"I do not have bones!" Victor said in a chipper tone.

Chubb laughed. "Dumbass A.I.! Oh! and this is Polpy. Don't make him angry." The large man tilted his head slightly and smiled. "Let's get this shit packed up. It smells terrible here. Robot! Help Polpy with the heavy stuff."

As the last crates of cargo were moved onto the ship, and the ARJACs were firmly locked in place, the ship took off, shaking Stasha's warehouse and bending the trees all around it. Victor stood in the cockpit, awaiting further orders.

Chubb complained about having to worry about keeping an android maintained and Polpy just sat in the copilot seat and listened.

Victor stood behind them, contemplating killing them right then and there.

Victor stood in a small conference room in front of Chubb, Polpy, and Grisly. It was similar to Stasha's kitchen. The room was roughly a square in shape, with a diameter of a few brisk steps. A pull-down curtain hung over the window overlooking the ARJAC storage bay. A projector loosely dangled from the ceiling, with wires creating a web around it. A small oval table in the center of the room was starting to rust. The chairs were in no better shape. Maps rolled into tubes poked out of every cabinet, with small tags on the tips saying what they were. Some were well known merchant routes within the solar sector, and others were singular planets. An old coffee machine sat in the corner on a small counter top. The entire area was stained with what looked like coffee.

Who would spill their coffee directly after making it?

They were looking him over, each with their own ideas for what to do with the fresh canvas. "He needs to be painted bright orange, since he's a maintenance android." Grisly suggested smartly.

Oh no. I don't want to be bright orange, Victor. Kill them before they do that.

"That's stupid and plain." Chubb scoffed "He needs to be spiced up with flames and cool emblems that signify how badass we are."

Okay, that's even worse an idea.

Polpy stood and watched the two girls argue. Coxswain sauntered in, slicking his hair back. "He should be left alone until he earns his marks. Think of the bounty hunters from Purmancia. When a kill is deemed significant, they add a tattoo symbolizing it." He stood proudly at his magnificent idea.

Now, I do like that idea. Fascinating people, those bounty hunters.

"But this is a repair android." The girls said in unison.

"Right," Coxswain averted his eyes awkwardly.

Polpy walked over to a nearby repair bench and grabbed an oily bandanna. He wrapped it around Victor's head. He motioned for the idea of clothing, rather than paint. The three looked at each other, nodded, and went to their rooms to find a piece of clothing to put on Victor.

After a few minutes of listening to people rummage through their clothing, they all appeared back in the room at the same time. Polpy came back with a pair of overalls, Chubb had a jean jacket with the arms cut off, Grisly with a military olive drab t-shirt, and Coxswain with a watch cap and a pair of classic sneakers.

Oh no. I hope they don't use all of it.

After an hour of Victor putting on and taking off various articles of clothing as well as multiple runs back to their respective rooms, Victor's outfit was decided.

He wore a black watch cap, a simple black long sleeve t-shirt, dark denim fitted pants, and Coxswain's classic sneakers.

Not gonna lie, this doesn't look half bad. Still wish we had Stasha's jacket. That would really put this outfit together.

"Thank you for the new clothing, shall I go to work now?" Victor asked in monotone.

The four looked at each other and then at the clock. It was already late into the afternoon. "Don't worry about it Arjie, we have no urgent repairs to do. You start tomorrow!" Coxswain clapped Victor on the shoulder and walked back to his room. The rest followed his example.

The first few days of Victor's infiltration were boring and monotonous. He mainly spent the days walking around the ARJAC hangar doing routine checks. None of them were damaged in any way, so he checked them twice a day to keep himself occupied. He had started to develop a routine.

First, he would check Chubb's ARJAC, since it was closest to the entrance into the ARJAC hangar. It was a bright blue bantamweight with red painted words. After checking all the systems, Victor read every word or sentence written on the hull. From top left to bottom right, like a book it read:

Eat shit! Suck on these fists. From Chubb, with hate and *STEALTH THIS BITCH.*

Then came Coxswain's ARJAC. His ARJAC was a dull gray tone welterweight. A large disc was mounted from the nape of the ARJAC's neck that hung above the head like a hat. After inspecting the ARJAC Victor found it to be a heavy, long range radar scanner.

It seems like Stasha built that radar dish herself from scratch. I've never seen anything like it. Ancient looking but probably triple the output of a standard ARJAC radar.

Third was Grisly's welterweight ARJAC. An old camouflage net hung on it's broad, rounded shoulders. The ARJAC was painted in a way that looked like a deer's fur, with white specks to look like spots of sun within a shaded area. Victor breezed past Grisly's ARJAC as it was the most plain, but seemingly also the most effective.

Last was Polpy's white, spider-like ARJAC. The four, sharp legs pierced the ground it stood on. The only cruiserweight within the Demolition Proxy's inventory. The lens on its head vacantly stared through Victor as he made his way over to it. The single eye somehow made it more uncanny compared to some other ARJACs that had multiple viewing lenses. Victor quickly passed over it. It still gave him a weird feeling every time he looked at it. Something just didn't look right.

Victor had just about finished up preparing the ARJACs for a deployment when Coxswain sauntered over to him and put his arm around him.

"Yo! Arjie! I got a favor to ask ya." He led Victor to his ARJAC with the big radar dish. "What's your real name?"

"I'm sorry sir, I do not understand the nature of your question. I am Arjie, I am here for repairs."

Does he know? Kill him.

"Look mate, I've been keeping an eye on you since

you got here. I've been combing over your movement with a fine brush. You have habits. Androids don't have habits."

Victor stopped his acting "why are you telling me this Coxswain? I can kill you right now."

"Because I know you won't. You want to know how I found out you weren't an android right? Oh, and call me Sean," he chuckled, "The name's Sean Bitterham."

Kill him right now. We don't have time for this.

"I already told you the basics of how I know, and no, I haven't told anyone else."

"So you want my help with something?" Victor pieced together.

"Aye lad, you're smart. I'd love to hear your story but we can talk personally later. Right now I'm going to tell you my plan. I want these pirates dead just as much as you do, probably more."

I don't trust him.

"So we almost always bring a spare ARJAC when we go on raids, you're going to stow away in it."

"So what? I'm going to shoot them in the back?" Victor asked.

"No lad, you're just the contingency plan. I don't know your skills yet and I don't trust you," Coxswain spoke in that accent that didn't quite sound like he was born with it.

"I used to be a special operative for the Prol. I've been trained my whole life to pilot an ARJAC" Victor boasted.

"Yeah and I'm Penelope Kross. Look lad, last time I checked, the Prol would sooner throw organic bodies at the enemy, not manufacture some sentient killing machine," Coxswain chuckled. "At least you've got a sense of humor."

That wasn't a joke scumbag.

Chubb poked her head out of the doorway to the meeting room, "Hey big brain! The microwave isn't working again!"

They both froze. Coxswain calmly turned around and yelled back, echoing in the massive hangar "Is it plugged in?"

Chubb quickly vanished and reappeared. "Smart as always Coxswain." She paused and looked at the two talking. "You got a thing for robots? Damn, you can't even get a human to fall for you," She chuckled to herself. Then the microwave dinged and she disappeared again.

The silence held for a few seconds. "The raid we are planning on doing is dangerous," he spoke plainly, his accent minimal. "The Prol have a convoy of experimental ARJAC reactor systems that are being smuggled out of the solar system. We are going to stop it when it makes a refueling stop on Mars before it goes to who-knows-where."

"So how do you plan on killing your comrades?"

"Oh I'm not going to lift a finger, lad. I'm going to feed them wrong information. You see, I'm in charge of all the communication and long range radar, as you can tell." He pointed to his ARJAC. "By the time their short range radars pick up on the enemies, they'll be dead. Even if it's just a small escort force, there's no way these stupid pirates can stand up to trained soldiers."

That's not that bad a plan, for a pirate.

"So what would I do if this plan of yours fails?" Victor questioned. "Say your friends kill the escort and take the reactors. You think they'll think you purposefully fed them wrong information?"

He laughed, "Not a chance lad! I've been slightly messing up a little bit with every raid. Gotta be consistent eh?"

He's been planning this for a while.

"That only answered one question, *Sean*."

"If they do succeed and get everything back to base, then you can go about killing them your sneaky way. Oh, and you can kill me too."

"So it's a win, extra win for me then?" Victor hoped the pirate would stay true to his word.

"Bingo. You're a sharp lad."

The two did an impromptu handshake. "So when's the raid?" Victor asked.

"Tomorrow."

6

The shuttle doors hissed and compressed air filled the small hallway. Sean Bitterham shivered as the air pierced his clothes. After a few seconds the doors leading into the *Hummingbird* slid open and a grisled man gave Sean a welcoming smile.

"Welcome aboard recruit! How was your trip from Prometheus-4? I hear the weather is especially brutal around this season." The old man led Sean through the wide hallways filled with shuffling crew members. The overhead rails hummed as messenger robots hurried to their respective delivery areas. Everything was clean, neat, and shining. "I'll show you to your bunk, you'll be with the other newest member. He may look young, but he's one of the toughest bastards I've met."

The two walked in silence briefly, Sean was unsure what to say. "You've got a busy week ahead of you. I've been told we already have an assignment for someone of your caliber. Reconnaissance specialist, right?"

"Yessir!" Sean stiffly responded. "Top of my class in reconnaissance and troop command!" Sean wore his honors with pride. It was not easy to be top of the class at the facilities of Prometheus-4. From birth, children were put through rigorous training to determine if they were capable of being a Steel Soldier. Harsh winters were dreaded by the trainees and celebrated by the trainers. Survival "classes" were held away from the facility buildings. Children were brought to the barren tundras and dropped off in packs. Very few flora and fauna lived in the survival training areas. They were even scarcer during the winter season, with anything that lived there dying or migrating. The only goal was to survive by any means and signal to be picked up when the shuttle flew overhead.

When Sean arrived at his small section of the massive ship, his bunkmate was already getting ready to leave. He was a well built blond man, with multiple scars across his back. He looked at Sean with a calm face, but his eyes were a raging inferno. "You're the new guy huh?" He scoffed. "Last new guy didn't even last a month." He put the rest of his black uniform on and pushed past Sean into the hallway.

"You'll get used to him eventually. He's always been like that. He has a thing against new guys. He had a..." The old man paused, "rather unfortunate accident that no one could save him from. He blames someone in particular." The old man pointed at one of the bunks, "This one's yours. It must be great to actually have blankets now. You can drop your stuff off here, I'll show you the dining area. It's almost breakfast after all. You must be hungry. Steel Soldiers always are."

Sean set his small bag down and followed the old man out of the room and down the hall. As they approached the dining area the hum of idle conversation filled the air. Warm, delicious smelling food flooded

Sean's nose. The cooking staff were hidden behind walls that only had slits to continue to fill the buffet areas. Two entire walls of the massive dining area were lined with different foods. Traditional foods from Earth, exotic foods from Vivladre, and even homemade recipes from the chefs. He stood in awe at the portions and quality of the food.

"This is going to be the best meal of my life," he muttered happily.

Sean took a lap around the dining area. Meat of all different seasonings marinated in the troughs, begging to be chosen. Salads sprouted from the bar, acting as a landscape of art for everyone dining. He did another lap, took a tray and decided what to eat. After getting a heaping helping of different meats and very few leafy greens, Sean looked for the old man, who had already gotten his food and started to blend in with the crowd. He waved to Sean from across the expansive room. The old man, the blond man, and a gentle looking woman sat next to a small porthole window.

"You seem to be quite the eater!" The woman exclaimed as she took a sausage from Sean's tray. Surprised, he looked at her and then everyone else at the table.

"She does that with everyone here," the old man chuckled. "Consider it bonding or something like it."

The blond man just stared into space and slowly ate his food, ignoring everything around him.

"Sir, you mentioned I had a special mission already

lined up?" Sean questioned. "When is the briefing?"

"It's later today, right after morning training and lunch. And no need to act so formal, kid, not around us, anyway." Sean quickly saluted. "And don't you dare say 'yes sir' right now," the old man interrupted jokingly.

Sean stopped saluting and nodded, "Aye."

"Your accent, how did you acquire it? Prometheus-4 is a training-from-birth planet." The woman asked.

"I figured out a way to hack into the communications tower without any way to trace it back. I would watch movies and newsreels from Purmancia," Sean recalled. "Since the instructors don't speak to you once you can read, I didn't have much trouble hiding it. The other lads in training saw it as a defining feature and they just started following me. I became something like a leader to them."

"You'll have no trouble getting a crowd to tell war stories" the woman said. The three chuckled.

"Speaking of war stories, have you heard about the Battle of Vivaldre?" the old man asked.

"DON'T tell that story again" the blond man said bitterly.

"Perhaps another time, then," the veteran chuckled.

Morning training went terribly for Sean. The four did some basic familiarity exercises and went over code words. The last section of morning training was the "blow off steam" section where they split into two teams and battled until one team was victorious. Of course, Sean's team was destroyed very quickly at the hands of two veteran Steel Soldiers.

Then came the briefing.

The old man and Sean sat in a small auditorium. The projector screen was turned off and there was no hint of it being turned on any time soon. The old man stared at Sean. His face turned extremely serious.

"Look kid. We brought you here to get one of ours back. He ejected a few years ago and we tracked his course. If all our A.I. calculations are correct, he's going to land on Earth in about five years. He's in hyperstasis so he should be fine. Theoretically. Your job is to get him back to us. Or at least tell us he's okay. Once we hear back from you, we'll decide what to do from there."

"I'm going undercover? How long?"

"Until we call you back, or you call us saying you found him." The old man relaxed a little. "Think of it as a vacation."

"So who am I infiltrating? Or is this an extended solo mission?" Sean dreaded years on end with no one to talk to.

"Relax kid, you'll be with people. I don't know if they'll like you though. We've done our research and they're a rowdy bunch."

"Mercenaries? Rebels?" Sean wondered.

"Pirates. They call themselves the 'Demolition Proxy.' Fancy name for a bunch of no ones stealing shipments." The old man brought out a small datapad. "This is the location of their main base of operations."

"That's on Earth's moon though!"

"Kross is too busy with her rebellion to take out small pirate factions. The Earth police force seems to be caught up with keeping the peace planetside so you should have an easy time making contact."

"So how do I find the lad you're looking for?" Sean asked.

The old man scrolled through the datapad. He brought up a profile of a young looking man with dark hair. "This is the profile for our missing guy. He didn't last long here but he was an amazing Steel Soldier and we can't risk him leaking any information about us as well. In the profile you'll find his habits, how he talks, how he walks, the whole picture. Study it well before you leave. He may look different now than in here."

"When *do* I leave, sir?" Sean was anxious to prove his worth.

"You leave in three days. Best get studyin' kid." The old man got up and clapped Sean on the shoulder. He turned around in the doorway and beckoned to Sean. "Come on, I can at least help you until dinner time."

Sean studied the datapad during every minute of

free time that he had. He went over camera footage of the missing man, his speech patterns, his ARJAC piloting tendencies, and even eating habits. When the time came to go out to find him, Sean was ready.

"What's the name of the lad I'm looking for?" Sean asked the old man.

"Sorry kid, we can't tell you that. He may be a part of our squad's history but it's still information I can't give you." Sean nodded and boarded his small, personal shuttle. "You'll need an alias. All the pirates have some weird name they call themselves. How about Coxswain? Since you're such an expert flyer." The old man suggested.

"I don't fly often."

"You're still better than most of the galaxy, you'll do fine kid!" The old man pressed a button to close the shuttle doors. The compressed air hissed as the shuttle became space worthy. Sean had a long trip ahead of him. He only had food, his wits, and a thin blanket to keep warm during his "night phase." Hyperstasis was not allowed because of the territory and speed of the shuttle.

The trip was silent. Sean didn't say a word as he drifted alone in the barren void of space. Months went by without a single word being uttered from Sean's lips.

"Unknown shuttle state your course and business." A gruff woman's voice crackled over the long range radio. "You are trespassing on Demolition Proxy territory. You are already subject to pay a fine before leaving or we will use lethal force."

"Oh shut up with the formal crap!" A terse woman's voice interrupted. "Dock with us and give us your money or we'll shoot you down!"

Sean "Coxswain" Bitterham woke up from his drowsy state. "It seems like I've reached the right place." He replied over the radio, his voice a husk of what it once was. "I heard you lads could use an operator and a better pilot."

"Shut up and land!" The terse woman shouted.

Coxswain deftly maneuvered the shuttle through the asteroid field created from the detonation of the dark side of the moon. Asteroids the size of men clumped together in walls to block him.

Upon landing in the hangar, two ARJACs pointed their Gauss Rifles at the ship. A short, round woman stood in front of the door. The shuttle door wheezed open. Coxswain stood in the opening, bearded and disheveled.

"I flew a long way to talk to you lads," He said with a drowsy mirth. "So can I join you friendly folks?"

"Where's my money?" The short, terse woman demanded.

"All I have are the clothes on my back and some spare rations, sorry lass. I came here for a job. The name's Coxswain, nice to work with ya."

"Coxswain? We don't need a pilot! We already have one!" The terse woman pointed her sidearm at Coxswain.

"Hold on there Chubb! Take a look at his shuttle."

The gruff woman's voice boomed through the ARJAC speakers. "It doesn't have a single dent. We always hit something when we get back to base. He has never been here before and made it through everything with almost no damage.

The ARJAC's chest opened up and a well built woman climbed down and briskly walked over to Coxswain. She looked over the shuttle with a keen eye. She circled it multiple times before finally facing him. "You fly?"

"Aye."

"You fly well?"

"Aye," he said with more confidence.

"Can you kill a man and take his shoes?" the well built women asked through a smile.

"I suppose I could, never stole his shoes though."

She looked Coxswain over and chuckled. "Man, your clothes are shit."

"I've been in there for a while, lass. Not much you can clean with."

She laughed heartily. "You're going to have to steal a dead man's shoes then!"

Coxswain laughed along with her, "When's the earliest I can?"

She nodded towards Chubb and the other ARJAC,

and they nodded back. "Welcome aboard. We could surely use you, but you have to earn your keep." They shook hands with a tight grip.

Coxswain smiled, "I can do that, lass."

7

"Preparations are complete ma'am," Victor said to Grisly in a robotic monotone. He handed her the datapad regarding her ARJAC. Victor had tampered with her short range radar systems enough that she shouldn't be able to see enemy blips until they were within firing range. The datapad showed that everything was in perfect condition.

"Damn, Stasha really sent us a good present this time. Works for nothing, doesn't complain, doesn't need breaks." Grisly thought out loud.

I need breaks you know. I'll hack your ARJAC.

"Easy there Arjie." Victor mumbled.

"Did you say something?"

"No ma'am. You may be having auditory hallucinations. I suggest rest." Victor covered for himself.

"Wish I could, but we have a convoy to butcher!" Grisly climbed into her ARJAC and prepared for the transport shuttle to take her away.

Chubb arrived in the hangar next. She stomped over to Victor. "Yo rusty! Everything ready?" She pointed at her ARJAC. She had written a new vulgar phrase on it. On her own personal Gauss Rifle. It used to be a regular steel, but now it was bright red with *Caution: Dead end ahead* in bold black letters.

"Yes ma'am," Victor replied in his usual monotone way. For Chubb's ARJAC, he tampered with the cooling systems so that when she inevitably used long bursts, her Gauss Rifle would overheat and possibly melt, leading to a horrible misfire. "All things are prepped and ready for action."

"Good." She pushed her way past Victor and quickly clambered up into the cockpit and waited for the shuttle.

Polpy lazily walked past Victor and gave him a questioning face and a thumbs up. "All things are in order sir," Victor replied instinctually. Since Polpy's ARJAC had four legs instead of two, Victor decided to tamper with the central gyroscope system. Without the full power of the CGS, quadruped ARJACs have a very hard time staying standing when moving over rough terrain or taking a hard hit. Polpy deftly climbed into his machine and silently waited for the time of the raid.

Coxswain sauntered in with his usual swagger. He put his arm around Victor, "I take it you've done your own preparations? I've done everything on my end that I can."

"Why do you trust me Coxswain?" Victor harshly asked. "You don't even know my name.

"They didn't let me know your name lad, but I was sent out to find you." Coxswain laughed. "I've been studying you since before you even knew about my existence."

What? Victor, this guy just gets weirder and weirder. We should just kill him with the rest.

"How did you know I wasn't just an android? If you don't tell me I'll kill you along with the rest of these pirates."

Coxswain went silent for almost a minute. His head swaying from side to side occasionally as he weighed his options. "Alright lad. You don't have to believe me on this but I'll tell you what I know. They kept a lot of things secret from me. I'm a soldier from Prometheus-4. My mission is to find someone that went missing years ago. I've studied and memorized with your exact mannerisms, lad. They didn't tell me your name but they showed me every video and data log they had on you. I can, without a doubt, say you're the lost Steel Soldier I've been sent to find."

Victor stood frozen. He looked into Sean's eyes "What was your base of operations?" Victor asked in a cold tone.

"I was on board the *Hummingbird* for about a week. I didn't get to know any names."

"Who was your commanding officer? Or since you didn't catch names, what did they look like?" Victor pressed.

"The man calling the shots for me was an old man, lots of scars, white hair, and a scruffy looking beard," Sean remembered. "It's been quite a few years since I left there lad, my memory might not be all that correct."

"No," Victor assured him. "You're remembering correctly." Victor weakly chuckled. "Looks like you were my replacement."

Victor, he could just be making this up and flying by the seat of his pants. Those were some pretty vague descriptions. He must've done his research on prominent Prol warships though. Keep asking him questions. I still don't trust him.

Victor thought for a moment, coming up with scenarios and questions in his head. "What did *I* look like?"

"You were a young lad, pretty well built. You had dark hair, clean shaven. Quite the babyface if you asked me." Sean laughed a little bit.

"And what about the other members of the squad? You must've met them." Victor pressured.

Sean put his hand on his chin and thought. "Hmmm. There was an angry blond lad-"

"So he's alive." Victor interrupted.

"And also a nice looking older lass. She and the old man seemed quite friendly."

"Did she steal some food from you?"

"Every day, during breakfast."

"She hasn't changed a bit!" Victor laughed, then

Sean joined in.

"Those are the Nightcats alright. So were you Nightcat four or did they give you another number?"

"I never officially became one. They only shipped me off with the callsign 'Coxswain.' I've been here ever since, looking for you lad." Sean looked back towards his ARJAC and the transport shuttle. "I should get going, they're probably getting antsy in there. You know my plan, whether you follow it or not is up to you lad." He turned and made his way to the shuttle.

"My name is Victor by the way. I don't have a last name. Is that something new that the Prol are doing for their Steel Soldiers?"

Sean turned and winked at Victor. "They give you your first name, so why not give yourself your last name?" He hurried to the shuttle and opened the massive hatch with a push of a button. He then climbed into his own ARJAC as the hatch opened, landing with a bang on the hard flooring. One by one, the massive war machines walked into the shuttle and held onto a large railing.

"Arjie!" Sean's voice boomed from inside his ARJAC. "Can you load up one of the spares? Who knows what trouble we'll get into."

Victor deftly climbed one of the spare ARJACs with enough robotic movement to possibly fool someone from far away. The ARJAC came with a standard GR-1 and one missile pod on the left shoulder carrying eight guided missiles. Victor climbed aboard the shuttle and secured his footing next to Sean's ARJAC. Sean gave everyone a thumbs up and locked his ARJAC's axis. He climbed out of the cockpit and walked over to the hatch lever inside the shuttle. He held the lever up until the hatch closed with a creak.

So you didn't end up tampering with his ARJAC?

"No... And good thing I didn't, he's on our side. There's no way he can guess four people's appearances without any wrong information. Not to mention Kali's food stealing habits."

You're right. But why is he working with the pirates?

Victor paused and thought. "Maybe they saw me all those years ago and calculated my course. I have no idea how they saw me. Was there a tracker on my old ARJAC?"

I am unsure. If there was one, it was not connected to the central control. I sent out pulses to say where we were, maybe it amplified them enough for a couple calculatory scans.

"What do you think Arjie? If he's here to take us back to the Nightcats, should we go with him? We can go back to them. They care enough to send someone all the way out here just to find us."

But why? We're just one man. We don't even have vital information about anything but standard Steel Soldier training.

The shuttle shook as it entered the atmosphere of Mars. Dust pelted the belly. Small rocks clinked off of the thick armored hull, causing a discordant rhythm of wind and Earthy violence. Sean's voice came over the intercom "We're landing in a dust storm. It's dangerous but it will give us plenty of visual cover from the convoy. Brace yourselves, lads it's gonna be a bumpy landing!" The shuttle slammed into the surface. Anything not nailed down was rocked into a cacophony of ringing metal. The ship left a small smokey crater. A couple minutes later Sean came back into the ARJAC storage on the shuttle with a breathing suit on. "We made it! No major damage to landing systems or anything else. We're good to go lads."

He pulled the hatch lever and held it in the downward position. Dust whipped in from the opening at the top as the hatch slowly descended into the sand. More and more entered the shuttle and the winds started shaking the ARJACs. Sean quickly ran to his ARJAC and climbed inside.

Chubb took the lead and pushed the hatch down the rest of the way. It landed with an unenthusiastic thud. The other three followed her outside into the storm. Sean glanced back at Victor, sitting motionless in his ARJAC and gave him a slight nod. The plan had begun.

"Just another few minutes or so and we'll be out of the storm and within visual distance of the convoy!" Sean informed the other pirates of the situation. They had been in the storm for almost twenty minutes, walking continuously. "Polpy, are you okay back there?"

His four legged ARJAC staggered in the wind and sand. He trudged along silently. Sean's radar had already picked up the convoy's position. There seemed to be about three or four guards, with only one large transport shuttle.

The storm started to clear, Chubb emerged from the wall of dust first. Her radio crackled "There's no transport shuttle! It's just a-" her radio went silent. The other three pirates emerged from the sand to see Chubb's ARJAC with a massive hole through the chest. Some kind of weapon shot clean through the cockpit. No sign of Chubb's body was even left.

Standing in front of the pirates was a black ARJAC. It looked too big and bulky to be called a cruiserweight. It was something *bigger.* It stood motionless with no ranged weapons. It held a two handed ax with its shaft digging into the sand. Its armor was rounded but not bulbous. A small shield was fixed in position on each of its arms.

On a faraway dune stood the silhouette of a quadruped ARJAC with thick legs. Instead of standard missile pods on the shoulders, the welterweight ARJAC had something Sean had never seen before. It looked like a matter cannon, but it was far too small. The hands of the ARJAC were free, but mounted on each forearm was a rotary machine gun.

Polpy saw Chubb's wreck and looked at the quadruped ARJAC. He screamed and charged it. The ax wielding ARJAC quickly sidestepped and blocked his path, pushing him back. The black ARJAC beckoned for Polpy to try again. Polpy threw his Gauss Rifle at the ARJAC and charged again.

The two collided and a shockwave of dust rippled

over the dunes. The black ARJAC fell backwards into the sand. Polpy climbed on top of it and started stabbing it with his spider-like legs. Every stab shrieked with metal-on-metal. Sparks flew with every hit. The black ARJAC's armor withstood every attack as it held the raging white spider at bay. It deflected one of the stabs with a shield, and a leg was stuck in the sand. The black ARJAC quickly grabbed the leg and threw the flailing monster into a sand dune. It stood up, grabbed its ax, and turned to face Polpy, who was struggling to stand.

It walked slowly towards the flailing white limbs now covered in scrapes, savoring the kill. The black ARJAC stomped on one of the spider-like legs to hold Polpy in place. It raised its ax above its head and swung downward. Polpy let out another roar as his ARJAC was cleaved in two.

Grisly opened fire on the black ARJAC, but her rounds seemed to have no effect. She aimed for the knees and managed to land a direct hit on the structure, leaving the ARJAC crippled and almost motionless. It looked at Grisly and she could feel the hatred radiating from the pilot. The ARJAC shook its head slowly.

Without warning, Grisly flew backwards and landed against a rock that stuck out of the endless sand. The outline of an ARJAC stood where Grisly had just been. The outline slowly gained color from its chest outward, like ripples in a still body of water. The ARJAC standing there was another black ARJAC with what seemed like standard weaponry. It had a device on its back that looked like some sort of backpack. The ARJAC disengaged the locks on the device and shrugged it off. It picked it up and tossed it to the ax wielding ARJAC. It shot a single round into Grisly's ARJAC, but it did not penetrate. Grisly stood up and beat her chest.

"Come on!" She yelled "I'm ready. Are you?"

The ARJAC replied with another shot in the exact same spot. This time it pierced Grisly's armor and her ARJAC stood motionless before dropping its Gauss Rifle into the sand. Grisly fell to the side, her cockpit flooding with red dust.

Sean recognized these ARJACs. He remembered seeing them years ago on a massive ship. He was only there a week but he remembered these ARJACs vividly.

"Sean!" Victor's voice crackled through the dust storm. "Those are not standard Prol ARJACs." The ARJAC turned its attention to Sean. "Sean, you need to survive until I get there. I'm coming as fast as I can. Those have to be the Nightcats!"

Sean turned and bolted to the nearest rock that he could use as cover. He kicked up sand and dust to try to blind the Nightcats, but with little success. The quadruped on the sand dune locked into his ARJAC and shot a piercing blow to his radar system. Sean ducked behind the red rock and checked his scanners. Nothing. All the sensors were offline, no communications either.

"Hold on there lads! It's Coxswain!" He tried to use the ARJAC's external speakers to hail the Nightcats. "This is serial number SC five, two, seven. It's Sean, hold your fire!" The dust storms were still raging, and it didn't seem like his words reached them. "Maybe I can use a hand signal or something."

He quickly stuck his hand out, waving in a panicked manner. It was promptly removed from his ARJAC by whatever weapon the quadruped was using. "Well I guess that's out of the question. Victor, you metal bastard, where are you?"

The rock shook as a couple shots penetrated into it. The shots were all in the same exact place, digging deeper and deeper into it. Eventually, a shot pierced the rock, and Sean's ARJAC. It grazed his side, sparks flying into the dusty air. The rock shook again, but there wasn't a shot this time. Sean quickly looked up to see the leader, the stealthy one, standing on top of the rock Sean was hiding behind.

He quickly kicked the rock, hoping to stagger the black ARJAC. Before his kick could land, the black ARJAC was already in the air, pouncing onto Sean. He was kicked in the chest, knocking him into the red sands. He scrambled to get on his feet, shooting his head mounted machine guns at any possible weak points he could think of.

Before he could fully stand, the black ARJAC punched Sean's ARJAC across the head, sending him reeling. Sean temporarily lost consciousness as he thudded into the sand. He woke up just in time to avoid an execution-style shot from the black ARJAC. Quickly jerking his head to the left, the round glanced past his shoulder and into the small crater where his head used to be.

Sean tried to shoot another burst from his machine guns, but the punch had damaged them, causing a misfire and explosion, rocking every fiber of his body. He swung a weak punch with his one working arm, but it was easily deflected.

Sean swept the feet of the black ARJAC. The hit landed, but while falling to the ground, it managed to land a crushing elbow blow to Sean's chest, severing the connection to the legs. Sean hit the ground hard rocking in his cockpit and blacking out again. When he came to, he couldn't move anything. The black ARJAC had pinned him to the ground with a foot on his chest, and a Gauss Rifle aimed directly at the cockpit.

A shot from behind Sean thudded into the sand next to the black ARJAC's foot. The two looked in the general direction of where the shot came from. Victor emerged from the dust storm, walking effortlessly through the sand. He held his hands up in a cautious manner. When he was clearly visible, he put his Gauss Rifle down.

Victor was shaking.

So you're up against three elite specialists that you know can easily beat you. You have no communications between you and you just SHOT at them.

"Arjie, there's nothing else I could've done to get their attention. I won't let Sean die like that. He should not die defenseless in the sand. That is not the way of Steel Soldiers."

So what do you have in mind to get them to not kill

you?

"I have no idea. I'm just winging it." Victor shot all of his missiles wide away from all the ARJACs now frozen, staring at him. "Arjie, turn up the volume of the speakers to maximum. I don't care if they break."

Sure thing. Done.

"This is Victor, of the Nightcats, serial number SC four one seven four. I know it's you in there Serge."

The black ARJAC pointed its Gauss Rifle at Victor.

Looks like they didn't hear you.

"I know what I have to do." Victor took the robot equivalent of a deep breath. "Arjie, open the cockpit."

Warning. Victor doing this will kill you. The Martian atmosphere is not breathable.

"I haven't been breathing in decades, Arjie. Open the hatch before they shoot me."

Who knows? Maybe you'll rust instead?

"Was that a laugh I just heard?" Victor took his helmet off and unplugged himself from the seat. "Open the damn hatch Arjie."

Opening cockpit now. No movement detected.

The hatch opened and Victor braced himself against the tearing winds. Dust and sand started to fill the cockpit. Victor shuffled to the edge of the hatch, holding on to the sides of the cockpit. He covered his eyes from the storm.

"Serge don't shoot!" Kali yelled over the radio. "That's Victor!"

Serge pulled back on his controls. "Are you sure, Kali? That's a robot. Why would that be Victor?"

"A robot doesn't shield his eyes," Rutri growled.

"Well at the very least, he clearly wants to talk. You should hear him out Serge." Kali pleaded. "You can't just shoot an unarmed pilot."

Serge nodded to himself. "You're right. It's not right to kill someone who can't even fight back." He threw his Gauss Rifle into the sand and took his foot off of the ARJAC he was pinning into the sand.

"Unidentified ARJACs, you have my attention. What do you want?" Serge listened for a response. "Kali, it looks like they can't hear us over the storm. I really hope we didn't kill anyone wanting to just talk. What if they were undercover agents? Command is gonna tear me a new one."

"Use Prol standard tactical hand signs." Rutri said.

Serge signed out "Who are you?" to the possible human-robot. He ran back into his cockpit and closed the hatch.

The plain ARJAC quickly turned on and signed "Victor, of the Nightcats" back to Serge. The three black ARJACs stood dumbfounded.

"It can't be." Kali was audibly in tears. "How can we have this much luck? It's been twenty six years since we lost him."

"I guess we know how his body lasted this long." Serge realized.

"It didn't," Rutri smugly remarked.

"Is it really you?" The black ARJAC signed back.

Looks like we got through to them.

"Can we talk where we can speak?" Victor signed. "We have a ship that way." Victor pointed behind him.

They could think this is a trap. Most likely they're going to ask for us to go to their ship.

Serge signed back "You come to us, we still need to be sure."

Victor laughed and gave a thumbs up. He strode to Sean and helped him up. Victor disconnected Sean's legs and carried him. The quadruped helped the cruiserweight walk. They followed the Nightcats back to their drop ship.

The walk was quiet. Sean coughed through the radio. "It's not looking good for me Victor. I'm not gonna make it lad."

He took quite a beating while you were getting to him. I'm surprised he's even still alive.

Victor shot his machine guns into the ground next

to one of the black ARJACs. They turned with weapons raised. "We need to hurry." Victor signed. The black ARJAC who fought Sean nodded and picked up the pace.

Sean's breathing was growing shallow, but he occasionally checked in with Victor, reassuring him he was still alive and conscious.

The black ARJACs stopped walking. Victor quickly scanned the area. There was no dropship. There were only a few large rocks, windswept by something recently. The angle was all wrong. It looked like the wind came from the center of the rough circle of moonstones. Suddenly, it appeared with the same style of optical camouflage that the ARJAC had been using. The doors opened, letting in the storm. They quickly walked in.

The giant doors closed, shaking the ship. The black ARJACs stood and watched as the two ragged pilots disembarked from their equally ragged ARJACs. Victor helped Sean out of the cockpit, his blood dripping onto the cold metal floor.

"Get a medic!" Serge's voice boomed and echoed in the dropship. His cockpit opened and he rushed to help stabilize the wound as best as he could. His hair was almost white now but it was still cut short like he had it all those years ago. Something about Serge's body seemed wrong to Victor. It was almost comforting in a way he couldn't place.

Kali docked her ARJAC and then rushed over to help. Her radiance was overwhelming. Her entire being glowed with a warmth Victor could only remember in scraps. Her hair was starting to gray, but its sheen darkness remained.

Rutri docked his ARJAC and left to get food for himself.

"I see the lad hasn't changed much." Sean coughed. Blood was starting to pool around where Sean was laying. Victor held his head up while Serge and Kali tried to prevent any further blood loss. The medics rushed over and pushed away the Nightcats.

"You better live through this. I owe you one for shooting you." Kali joked through her nervous breaths. "I won't steal your sausages anymore I promise."

Victor, Kali, and Serge walked in silence to the small mess hall inside the dropship. Serge and Kali studied Victor as he stared at them blankly. Serge took a sip of an unknown mixture of hard alcohols. "So you're really alive. Huh." He leaned forward and inspected Victor closer. "How?"

"I would hardly call this living." Victor's voice was metallic. "I still feel like a ghost. Or that this is all some kind of dream." He looked down on himself, inspecting what his perspective could see of himself.

"How did you get like this though?" Kali asked, her voice was like a mother asking about an injury that their child had at school.

"It was all thanks to Stasha." Victor replied with a melancholy kindness in his voice. "I don't know how she did it, but she told me she managed to transfer my brainwaves into this body." He gestured to himself, "All I remember is this feeling of absolute despair and darkness. I thought I was already in Hell. Then. I was awake in a brightly lit room. She showed me the escape pod, she showed me. *me.*" Victor paused and hung his head briefly. "I SAW myself and what I looked like after all those years stuck in hyperstasis. It wasn't good. I killed myself. This is all that's left of Victor. I can't be left alone with myself. I don't feel human anymore."

Victor looked at the two longingly. "I don't know what to do."

I've changed too.

Kali put her hand on Victor's cold shoulder. She looked into his eyes and smiled, tearing up. "You're home now. You're with us again."

Serge had his arms crossed, eyes closed. He nodded solemnly.

"I have to go back to Stasha. She deserves to know I'm okay. You wouldn't have found us if I wasn't helping her deal with the pirates." Victor pleaded.

"Those were pirates? Oh, I was worried I had killed your friends!" Serge exclaimed in a joking manner that seemed almost like worry.

The group chuckled slightly. "That was the Demolition Proxy, they had Stasha under their thumb for years. I'm glad she's finally free now. I need to tell her!"

"Once we hear back from the medic about Sean's

condition we can go get her. Where is she? On Mars?" Serge asked.

"Earth."

Serge almost spat his drink onto the table. "Earth? We can't go there! That's the homeworld of the rebellion!"

"And I know the ways in and out. They're too preoccupied with pirates and their own internal affairs to worry about one measly ARJAC dropship." Victor leaned forward. "I need to go to Stasha, I can't have her worrying any more than she already has been."

A low ranking officer approached the table and saluted. "Sir, Sean is stable. You may see him now."

"Thank you, you may go." Serge stood up. "Shall we see our mutual friend, Victor?"

"It doesn't look too bad, does it?" Sean looked over his new metal leg with a glossy stare.

Kali gently put her hand on his arm. "It looks fine, you'll be wearing pants most of the time anyway, no one will see it."

Serge and Victor were just inside the doorway. Serge had his arms crossed and was leaning against the medical cabinet. Victor had his hands inside of a worn jacket that Serge had given him.

Victor nodded at Sean, "At least you managed to get away with only a prosthetic leg. I'd say you're lucky that the doctors treated you at all, but you earned that right in their eyes."

"I also got a lot of my insides replaced, lad. It's not all roses and sausages." He patted his stomach with a soft, melancholic hand.

A doctor pushed past Serge and Victor. "You've had your time with him, he needs to rest and let his body adjust to the new organs." The doctor looked at Victor, "Since when did you guys get personal assistant androids? Looks like a new model." He knocked on Victor's chest. "Playing dress-up too? You guys get all the breaks."

Please punch him.

Serge grabbed the doctor's wrist. "That isn't an android, and I suggest you get back to your own work," Serge spoke tersely. "If you want to continue to do what you do." Serge nodded to Kali and Victor. "Let's give our friend some rest.

Victor knocked on the doctor's chest jokingly. "Right behind you sir."

The three walked out of the medical facilities.

"Oh, and Victor?" Serge asked. "I'll prepare a shuttle for you. Just you going down there?"

"Yessir, unless you want to meet Stasha." Victor's voice seemed to perk up slightly.

"Well we don't make one person shuttles so I suppose we might as well use the space," Serge added. "I'd love to meet the woman who saved your ass. It should be ready by tomorrow."

8

Victor, Kali, and Serge buckled themselves into adjacent seats in the massive shuttle. The smallest one they had could carry twenty troops. Rather than twenty nervous soldiers, only three excited people sat next to each other, making the monochrome cube seem more empty, more free. The remaining seats were folded up on themselves.

The trip was relatively short, considering the *Hummingbird* was orbiting Mars. Victor was anxious to see Stasha, it had been weeks since they had even spoken. He somehow felt butterflies.

Victor, I am simulating standard human "gut feelings" based on your emotional state.

"Thanks." He leaned back in the constricting seat.

The shuttle landed smoothly, and Victor heard the familiar sound of Stasha's workshop doors closing overhead. He quickly unfastened himself from his seat and rushed to open the door. It hissed and opened slowly. The wait was agonizing.

Stasha stood with one hand on her hip, the other holding a power drill. "Took you long enough!" She shouted over the powering down of the engines. "I've been working on something special for ya!" She beckoned for Victor to follow her, but stopped when Serge and Kali entered the shuttle's doorway. "Who are they?"

"Friends from before all this." Victor motioned to himself. "You can trust them."

Stasha glared at them and tapped her foot, thinking. "Fine, but no guns. Leave them where you stand."

"Fair enough." Serge agreed as he took out his sidearm and placed it in the doorway. Kali did the same.

The three followed Stasha into her kitchen. "She makes really good coffee, you should try it." Victor recommended.

"Oh how would you know, all you do is eat air." Stasha laughed. "They'll see for themselves how good it is. True earth coffee, classical." She poured out a couple cups, the steaming liquid sloshing in the homely mugs.

They sat around Stasha's small worn out table, using worn out cups and mugs to drink the coffee. Serge took a sip of the steaming liquid and raised his eyebrows in approval. "This is definitely better than anything I've tasted."

"It's homegrown. Everything you're drinking came from right outside. Well, the greenhouse is right outside." She was elated to finally share her fruits of labor.

"When did you get that? It was just the warehouse

when I left," Victor asked.

"You never had a need to see it," Stasha shrugged.

"You live out here alone? Isn't it boring?" Kali leaned forward, holding her coffee with both hands, occasionally sipping.

"Well I like to keep myself busy. Projects are a great way to do that. The greenhouse only took a month to build. It wasn't that hard. I spent this recent time on a thank-you present to Victor." She smiled as she put her head back in remembrance. "It really is my finest work. Unique, one of a kind."

"So when do we get to see it?" Victor questioned.

"When I've made you wait enough," Stasha laughed. "I worked my ass off to get this thing done. The least you could do is squirm for a little bit."

Serge finally spoke up, "Do you do everything here yourself? That must be a lot of work."

"Yeah. My parents died. Were killed when I was young." Stasha paused to regain her composure. "Luckily our mutual friend just got my revenge. Well, all the original pirates were long gone."

"The Demolition Proxy is now officially... Demolished." Victor joked.

That was a horrible joke and you know it.

"Never say that again." Kali and Stasha said simultaneously.

Victor chuckled. "Yes ma'ams."

"Hurry up and finish your damn coffee. It's almost time for the main event."

"Are you guys coming too?" Victor asked excitedly.

"Well if she built you, imagine what else she could do," Kali replied.

"I'd like to see something that isn't standard Prol tech." Serge shrugged jovially.

Stasha led them to the rear end of the giant warehouse. They walked past the shuttle, maneuvering around the landing gear.

Victor noticed the feet first but the shuttle still blocked his vertical vision. They were brand new, with a shimmering steel gray paint. As Victor excitedly pushed past to be the first to see it, he turned his gaze upwards.

The knees were well guarded, but left enough room for maneuverability. The hip rotors were exposed, with external armor from the thigh shielding them from most ballistic damage. It had two small rocket pods on either side of its head, resting on the collar. There were bigger hatches on each shoulder, but they didn't quite look like rocket pods.

Victor slowly circled the ARJAC. He didn't speak. He didn't even hear if anyone was talking to him. He made his way to the rear, and came into view of a high caliber, rotary machine gun mounted on the back. He then looked behind himself and noticed a strange gun with a hole in the top of it leaning against the wall.

"This is amazing!" Victor said in awe. "What's that?" He pointed at the gun bigger than a car.

". and it has integrated-" Stasha stopped. "You weren't listening were you? I'm gonna have to start my speech over again aren't I? That? That's not even the best part about this. That's just a AMC, generation two."

Victor stared blankly.

An ARJAC Matter Canon, Victor.

"Why does it have a hole in the top?"

Stasha turned to Serge. "Does he not know about the generation two's? He was around when they were in prototype."

Serge shook his head. "Classified info at the time."

"Generation twos only work with S-ARJACs. The 'S' stands for symbiotic. The arm of the ARJAC melds with the gun, making it more accurate as well as providing more weight control."

"Woah, Kali why don't you use these?"

"They don't have as much firepower as the standard matter canons. My ARJAC has four legs, making the weight of a standard matter canon bearable. The shoulder mount also helps," Kali chuckled. "Also mine is generation three."

Stasha quickly turned to Kali. "Wait the gen threes

are in active testing? I thought they were still in the theoretical state. This is big news. Can you give me any information on how they work?"

"That's classified Prol secrets." Kali winked.

"And what are these?" Victor pointed at the large hatches on the shoulders."

"Those are cooling vents. They open up when the ARJAC overheats. They also house a Personal ARJAC Stealth System, or PASS."

"Like Serge's backpack but integrated." Victor put his hand on his chin.

"Yes, but the backpacks are there for cooling purposes. PASS's are a high risk device, with heat so hot it can potentially melt the device, causing unwanted damage." Serge explained. "The hatches are a good idea, they can help alleviate some of the heat, even if it is just with air flow." He gave Stasha a thumbs up.

"So can I test it out?" Victor asked.

"Not yet," Stasha explained. "But we can set you as the active user." She paused briefly and then shouted, "Project!" The five eyes flickered yellow, then glowed constantly. The large center eye seemed to stare into Stasha's soul. "I am no longer the operator of Project, access code V7323."

"Access accepted," a deep robotic voice boomed and echoed throughout the warehouse. "Who is the new operator?"

Stasha motioned for Victor to say something.

"I am the new operator, I am Victor."

The ARJAC did nothing.

Access code, dumbass.

"Access code V7323."

"Operator accepted. Will you keep my name as Project?"

"For now, yes." Victor inspected the machine wryly.

"Very well," the ARJAC boomed.

"Arjie, I have an idea."

Yes, I already know what you're thinking. It can be done.

"So how do I get in?" Victor looked back and forth between Stasha and the ARJAC.

"Just get close to it." Stasha waved him toward it.

As Victor slowly approached the ARJAC, the upper torso unlatched, and rose. The small hatch in the middle opened downwards as a footstool. The ARJAC bent downwards and put its hand before Victor. He looked back at Stasha, Serge, and Kali.

"Well don't just look at me, get on it!" Stasha egged him on.

Victor hesitantly stepped onto the monstrous

hand. It slowly rose until Victor was standing right next to the hatch.

Now this. This is cool. I can't wait to try this out.

"Hush Arjie." Victor climbed into the cockpit and looked around. "It feels good to be back. Wait a minute!" Victor poked his head out of the ARJAC. "Stasha, did you use my old cockpit?"

"No, you destroyed that, but I DID model it after yours. Thought you'd find it easier to adjust that way. Since this is yours!" Stasha shouted back. Her voice was noticeably happier with the stress of such a massive project lifted off her shoulders.

A shadow quickly blocked out the sun overhead. The sound of engines filled the warehouse hangar. A voice boomed, filling the air with a familiar voice. "You have been conversing with a known Prol enemy. Victor, Serge, and Kali, of the special unit known as the Nightcats, you are under arrest for conspiracy and non-hostilities towards Stasha Kross."

9

Victor, I need roughly ten and a half seconds to connect myself and take over the ARJAC. I have formulated a plan. It gives everyone a slightly higher chance of survival.

"I'll stall them the best that I can. Or I guess try not to get shot." Victor quickly closed the cockpit hatch and started to switch everything on. The ARJAC flickered to life as he plugged into the systems.

The booming voice overhead was now accompanied by rappelling shock troopers. "Power down the ARJAC or we will be forced to shoot."

Five seconds left.

"Power down. Now."

Two.

A warning shot from the ship thumped between the ARJAC's legs.

Done. Powering down. Good luck out there.

"What do you mean 'Good luck' Arjie, aren't you coming with me?" Victor sprang up and quickly dismounted from the ARJAC. There was no time to argue. He trusted Arjie completely.

The shock troopers surrounded Victor, looking him over to make sure he matched the description that they were briefed on. They wore heavy gray armor all over their bodies. They might have been from the Iron Corps, but they were on the cusp of being promoted to Steel Soldiers. Each one of them was a specialized killing machine. Kali, Serge, and Stasha were also engulfed in shock troopers. They were forcibly restrained and bound, forced to their knees.

Victor shot a glance at Stasha, trying to get her attention to physically ask "why did you not tell me?" but she couldn't see him past the aggressive troops.

The looming ship had now landed during the scuffle, and the troops brought them on board. Stasha was shouting, "I have never been a part of the rebellion! I don't see my grandmother! I never asked to be born into this damn family!"

Stasha sat tied to a chair alone in a dark room. A bright light blinded her to anything past her feet. Her mouth trickled blood. She could barely keep her head up. It was throbbing and spinning at the same time.

"How long have I been here?" she thought. "Has it been weeks? Days? Hours? Minutes even?"

A slim blond man came into her vision. "I know you know where she is. Being the grandchild of an interstellar *hero*," he said the word with disgust.

Stasha shook her head. "Maybe at the beginning of

this beating I would've told you, if I knew where that bitch was. But then. well. just look at me. You're just as bad as she is." She spat the blood from her mouth.

"You know what they say." Stasha received a swift punch to the stomach. "The devil you know."

"That doesn't even make sense." Stasha slumped. "She cares more about the rebellion more than her own family. I haven't seen her since I was six."

"We'll try again later. Take her back to her cell."

Victor sat alone. His cell was not even a cell. They locked him in a storage closet close to the detention block. Arjie had uploaded himself to the ARJAC and managed to figure out a way to delete himself from Victor's mind. For the first time in Victor's memory he was truly alone. Arjie was gone.

He tried to make food appear like Arjie did, or have some form of drink, but nothing happened. "I guess I have the time to master it." Victor sat on an overturned box. "I have nothing but time. This whole *completely* alone thing is a little different though." He leaned back, resting hsi head on the metallic wall.

A faint rumble shook the ship. Footsteps pattered past Victor's door. Another rumble, much louder, rocked the ship. Alarms screamed in the halls. Soldiers shouted orders, muffled through the walls.

"Who's attacking us? Are they pirates?" Soldiers

were panicking in the halls.

"It can't be pirates, how stupid do you have to be to attack a Prol flagship?"

"Is it Kross?"

"Who the hell knows! Get to your stations!"

Victor started to hear a loud, rhythmic banging that seemed to be coming from outside the ship. The banging stopped right above Victor. It was all silent for a few seconds, then a Gauss Rifle fired two rounds, tearing through the ship and breaking open Victor's closet-cell.

Victor shot out of the cell and into open space. He slammed into beams and torn parts of the hull as he careened into nothingness. He was spiraling out of control just when an ARJAC grabbed him.

While enveloped in the ARJAC's hand, Victor was relieved that Arjie had come up with a plan that was risky, but worked out well in the end. The hand opened up and revealed a Prol standard issue ARJAC. It looked at Victor and he could see the small caliber machine guns locking onto him.

The ARJAC quickly turned around and was shredded by some kind of machine gun from the waist up. Victor was let go, spiraling into space again as the pilot was killed and lost control. He tried to see who had been shooting.

Victor's personal ARJAC pushed aside the floating scrap and swiveled its head, searching for Victor, its back mounted machine gun spinning wildly. Once it found him, it disengaged the magnets in its feet and thrusted towards him.

When it got close enough, it reengaged the magnets and stuck to the surface of the *Hummingbird*. It reached out a hand and the cockpit hatch opened to reveal an empty seat.

Victor grabbed hold of one of the fingers and was brought into the cockpit. He closed the hatch and sat down, plugging into the ARJAC systems. The hatch closed fully with a hiss and he could hear again.

Welcome back Victor, did you miss me?

"You had me worried for a second Arjie. How does it feel having a body of your own now?"

Not too different than when I was with you. Movement is the same, but shooting is completely new to me. I recommend being as one until I can master the controls.

"I don't have any other ARJAC to pilot so I might as well-"

Hostiles approaching.

"Right, we'll talk later." Victor turned to face three ARJACs. "So what's the situation, ammo, tactics?"

We have the AMC-2 and rear mounted rotary machine gun that Stasha installed. Also a reentry pack at seventy-four percent fuel. We require seventy percent for a safe entry.

"Okay, cut me off at seventy-one percent then."

Will do.

"Let's kick some ass."

Victor launched into space and fired a round from the AMC-2 into the nearest ARJAC. It tore through the entirety of it, as well as some of the hull of the *Hummingbird*. Unable to operate, the ARJAC drifted slowly into space. It listed almost gracefully. Victor engaged the reentry pack and plummeted back to the *Hummingbird*, denting the hull upon landing.

Seventy-two percent.

Victor spun up the machine gun, bringing it from its resting position to mounting it above his head. It whined, and let out a flurry of rounds, completely immobilizing the second ARJAC.

"These are some powerful guns!" He wasn't used to this level of firepower.

I stole some top-of-the-line anti-armor rounds for the machine gun, and matter canons are just that good.

"Remind me to ask Stasha about how they work."

Or I could just tell you after all this.

Victor jumped to his left to avoid oncoming fire from the third ARJAC.

More will be coming and you still need to get the others. Victor I am taking control. I will meet you back on Earth.

"Wait what?" Victor's controls no longer functioned. He tried to shoot at the last ARJAC, but nothing responded. Suddenly the AMC-2 fired and decimated the right shoulder of the ARJAC, killing the pilot.

"Not a very good shot still. Yeah you DO need practice."

The cockpit hatch opened again and Victor felt the tug of space. He disengaged the locks on his seat and disconnected from Arjie. He was pulled into the void again and quickly caught by Arjie's free hand. The massive machine deftly maneuvered to where the detention block was. Arjie jammed the barrel of the AMC-2 into the hull and fired, tearing a hole straight through the *Hummingbird*.

A Gauss Rifle round skimmed the leg of Arjie, and he quickly looked to see who had fired it. Two more ARJACs were on their way to deal with them. Arjie quickly looked at Victor and nodded.

"Oh no." Arjie reeled back. "No no no no no!" and threw Victor into the hole.

Victor crashed into a platform that had originally been the hall outside of the detention block. "We have to work on those if that's going to be a regular thing." He grabbed hold of a beam next to him and punched in the override command to open the door.

The door opened and air rushed out into space. Victor climbed into the doorway and closed the door. He turned to see two armed guards aiming at him. They had braced against an emergency railing.

"I was ejected into space. I am back now." Victor used his best android impression as he casually walked towards them.

The two hesitated just long enough for Victor to get within melee range. He punched one of them in the throat, seized the rifle they were holding, and shot the other guard in one fluid motion. The two guards collapsed to the floor, choking on their blood and gasping for air.

"Victor? How the hell did you get here?" Serge was locked up close to Victor's cleaning closet-cell. "I never saw you leave the closet."

"Long story short, I was shot out into space, and now I'm back."

Serge stood back, bewildered. "Well let's just get outta here and clear this up with everyone." He was worried, and Serge rarely showed those kinds of emotions.

"I don't think that's the plan, and I don't think that can happen." Victor explained. "Arjie may have destroyed most of the ship. He's uploaded himself into the ARJAC Stasha made."

"He can do that?" Stasha shouted from down the hall, a spark of energy returning to her voice.

"Let's just get you all out of here and back to Earth shall we?" Victor said as he unlocked Serge's cell door.

"You go get Kali, I'll get Stasha. Meet at the escape pods on the far end."

"Right." Serge made his way to Kali's cell while Victor jogged over to Stasha's cell.

"Victor, you have to let me analyze Arjie, and also how did he do it? Did you know?" Stasha had dried blood streaked across her face and clothes.

"I have a lot of questions for you too Ms. Kross," Victor scowled.

"I can explain when we get the hell outta here." Her excitement faded quickly at that mention.

"You should also see a doctor, you look beat." Victor pointed out.

"Well yeah, they don't take too kindly to people like me," Stasha retorted.

Victor helped Stasha down the hall and into the escape pod, where Serge and Kali were already waiting.

"So are you just going to leave without me lad? I thought we had a connection." Sean coughed from behind a cell door.

"Sean?" Kali gasped. "What are you doing down here?"

"I worked with Victor, and since he worked with Stasha, here I am. So are you going to let me out or?" They could hear the smile in his voice.

Victor hurried over to Sean as Serge, Kali, and Stasha climbed into the escape pods. Victor opened the door and carried Sean. Once they were seated and fastened in place, Serge hit the button to launch.

Serge looked out the small porthole window. "Damn you two did a number on that thing. I'd say it's pretty much useless."

"Then we don't really have much time." Kali explained, "The closest ship is in the system over, we have maybe a week or two before help arrives."

Arjie looked back from his fight to see the escape pod, and after calculating the trajectory, jumped off the *Hummingbird* and started reentry procedures following the same path.

Victor looked at the situation with optimism. "Then it looks like we get some time to make things turn in our favor."

The escape pod was silent. Everyone was coming up with their own plans for survival. Sean and Stasha tended to their wounds. The pod landed in a ghost town, smashing through ruins and husks of housing left abandoned for what looked like centuries.

The roads were overgrown with green shrubs and small trees. Rusted cars slouched on deflated wheels in driveways. Animals chittered as they fled from the impact site. Buildings shook, some walls collapsing from the shockwave of the crash.

"Where the hell are we?" Serge staggered out of the pod.

Victor turned to look at the small digital map in the pod dashboard. "It looks like... A place called Tazenakht. Stasha, you know where that is?"

"Haven't got a clue. I'm surprised the pod knows where we are." Stasha said as she climbed out of the pod, helping Sean.

A scorpion stung Victor's foot. Its tail bounced off the metal. The scorpion reeled back, rethinking its strategy to the invaders of its soil. Victor jumped after noticing the demonic looking insect. He kicked it, sending it flying into the sandy plain.

"I think we should get inside one of those buildings first, then plan our next move. We don't have too much time, we need to get somewhere that has more than just crumbling bricks." Victor quickly searched for the most intact building and hurried everyone inside.

"So how long until they find us?" Kali asked.

"I'd give it about a month, tops." Serge looked out of a broken window. "Maybe less if we stay here."

Something crashed outside, kicking dust into the air, blocking out the setting sun. Serge reached for his pistol, only to find his holster was empty. Everyone pushed up against a wall to try to hide from sight of whatever just landed outside.

Another crash, more dust. This one was closer than the other. Machine guns spun up and let loose a swarm of bullets. A deafening *boom* shook the bolts in Victor's body. Something began to fall. Its shadow made the room almost pitch black. Half a second later, it crashed through the ceiling, tearing out half the building in the process.

An ARJAC with a clean hole through the center of its torso was in front of them, sparks coming out of the slightly red cavity.

"I take it Arjie is here." Victor looked out of the crumbling building. "Yup. There he is." Victor waved at Arjie to get him to come over.

"Victor, a couple followed me down. I need your expertise if we are to succeed." Arjie's voice boomed with a sense of repetition in the statement.

"How long do we have until they arrive?" Victor asked.

Arjie quickly glanced at the sky, "Roughly one minute, maybe two."

"I'd rather save ammunition, is it possible to get everyone on board before they arrive?"

"Two others can fit in the cockpit, the rest will have to hold on the exterior."

"Let's get to it then! Sean and Stasha, you two are pretty beat up, you ride inside. Kali, Serge, you get the window seats." Victor wasn't used to taking command.

Something felt off about giving orders.

"How thoughtful," Serge retorted.

Victor helped Sean and Stasha into the cockpit and then climbed in, plugged in, and closed the hatch.

Welcome back Victor.

"I see you're back to your old ways of being in my head again."

Until you leave, yes.

Victor extended his left hand so that Serge and Kali could ride. They climbed on and held onto the fingers. An ARJAC crashed down behind them. Victor quickly charged his matter cannon and ripped a hole through the cockpit before the Prol pilot could react.

"We need to leave." Victor looked around. "Stasha do you have anything at your hideout that would prove useful?"

"I have an old ship that I inherited from my parents. Should be somewhere around my workshop." Stasha stopped and thought. "Are we anywhere near my workshop?"

"No," Arjie's voice softly spoke through Victor's body. "Your workshop is in Vaasa. It's quite a hike."

Victor shook. "Don't do that again." He briefly felt as if he were dreaming and not in control of his body.

There is an underwater tunnel on the northern coast,

I suggest starting with that. We should arrive there by nightfall.

"Arjie says there's a tunnel north, so we'll start there. I hope we can come across some food for you guys, it looks like it could be a few days or more before we get to Vaasa."

"How does the lad know that?" Sean weakly asked.

I mapped it out while crashing to Earth.

"He says he mapped it out while in space." Victor was relieved to be a middle man again.

Not what I said but close enough.

Victor turned North. "Hold on out there you two! It's going to get bumpy." And they were off.

Serge and Kali gripped the fingers of the ARJAC as tightly as they could while Victor started running at full speed, eager to be out of the ghost town.

Follow the coast when you get to the ocean.

There's the tunnel, we're about a tenth of the way to Vaasa.

"Look at the size of those windows!"

They passed a cathedral. Some colorful windows depicted epic moments in a long forgotten story were still intact. Its broken spires reached into the sky. Massive doors hung loosely on rusted hinges.

"Where are all the people?"

Nothing but ghost towns populated this area of Earth. Some were sprawling complexes, with toppled skyscrapers and buses. Others were just small towns ruined from time and neglect. Trees taller than Victor had ever seen surrounded an especially verdant patch of land.

"Okay who needs to stop for a break?"

Almost there.

Some time passed in silence, except for the thudding of Arjie's massive metal strides.

We are now in Vaasa.

"Okay, it looks like there are still quite a few Prol soldiers here. The only weapon we have is a loud-ass ARJAC. Do we have any plans?" Victor asked the group as they observed the workshop from afar. Dense tree cover made it almost impossible for untrained eyes to make out anything.

Stasha drew a map in the dirt for them. "So we're here, and the workshop is here, which would make the ship." She glanced back at the workshop. "About here. It's hidden under some trees and a camouflage tarp. It's far away enough that they might have missed it."

"Arjie you stay here, when you see or hear the engines start, come and meet us there," Victor instructed. "Also, make sure Sean is cozy in there."

Arjie gave a thumbs up.

The group circled around the workshop towards the ship. When they got there, they could see that the tarp was thrown to the ground and the ship was being guarded by a few soldiers. Two of them were talking with each other a little ways off.

Serge, Kali, and Victor looked over the situation and immediately came to an unspoken agreement on what they should do.

Kali diverted off to one side, making her way through the thick undergrowth. Serge and Victor went the opposite direction, making sure to be directly across from Kali and the soldiers.

A minute later, Kali stumbled into view, covered in dirt. She collapsed on the ground in sight of the soldiers.

"Isn't that one of the fugitives?" The guards looked at each other, confused.

"Are we supposed to take her alive or just kill her?"

Victor and Serge slowly approached the soldiers from behind.

"I don't remember, if we kill her and we aren't supposed to, we would be executed for disobeying such an important order."

"I'll call it in." The soldier fumbled with his radio. "This is Delta five two zero to command-"

Both of the soldiers were grabbed and their heads

twisted in ways that were only possible on owls. Their corpses fell without grace, dropped by Victor and Serge.

The radio crackled "What do you have to report?"

Victor quickly snatched the radio and played around with the tone of his voice to match the soldier. "One of the fugitives wandered into us, we shot her on the spot. Female, wearing a Prol uniform, somewhat older looking." Kali frowned, she wasn't older looking in her eyes.

"The others will be close by, we're sending you back-up. What is your location?" The radio asked.

"We are at the south side of the area. She came from the south as well." Victor was perfectly mimicking the dead guard.

"Roger that, we'll have the search crew do a sweep of that area again."

"That should buy us a little time." Victor said after he turned off the radio. "There's only one left so let's just get on the ship."

As the three were making their way to the ship, Stasha emerged from the brush and swiftly kicked the back of the soldier's leg, causing him to collapse. She then stabbed a sharpened branch into his neck. He fell to the ground, choking on his blood.

The three watched with amazement. "Why didn't you just use the knife you sharpened the stick with?" Serge asked.

"What knife? They took everything I had back on the big ship." Stasha cleaned her hands on her already bloodied overalls. "Are we getting in?" She motioned to her now-uncovered ship.

The three nodded in an approving disbelief. They picked up the rifles the soldiers were holding and boarded the ship. Stasha made her way to the cockpit and the intercom within the ship crackled "I'll keep the rear door open. Shoot back at anyone, ya hear?"

The engines roared to life and within a couple seconds Arjie was bounding over the workshop. The rotary machine gun was in full rotation, turning soldiers in the workshop into a red mist. The constant roar of bullets colliding with metal walls deafened the sprawling room. Prol soldiers were trying to communicate but it was no better than shouting at a dead man.

"Start taking off, I'll manage!" Arjie's voice shook the trees.

Stasha pulled up and the ship started to ascend. Arjie leaped and grabbed the end of the door. The ship shook and dipped. The three still in the cargo bay braced themselves against anything they could find. Arjie climbed up with some effort and flopped onto the floor with a screeching thud.

"Close up the door!" Kali said into the radio she was desperately holding onto.

The massive hydraulic door closed, sealing the ship with a hiss. Arjie opened the cockpit hatch with an internal command code. "Can someone get me off this ride? I don't think I'm tall enough to ride yet!" Sean weakly called from inside.

Victor helped him down and once Stasha had maneuvered into a safer part of space, she put it on autopilot and gathered everyone in the lounge. They almost stood shoulder to shoulder in the confined but comfortable space.

"So does anyone have a hideout that the Prol don't know about?" Stasha sharply asked, eager to leave the home system of humanity.

Everyone looked at each other. Serge snapped his fingers and lit up. "How about Vivaldre! We had a house there!" He motioned to Kali.

Kali shook her head, "We sold the house as we left remember?"

"Damn. That was a nice little bonus though," Serge said.

"How about Purmancia?" Sean casually questioned.

Stasha paced for a minute, muttering to herself. She checked an old interstellar map. "It checks out, plus with all the oddjobs living there we seem like we could fit in. It'll take a while to get there though."

"How long? I'm trying to get my hands dirty again." Victor threw his fist into his palm a couple times and shadowboxed playfully. "I don't want to be waiting around forever."

"Easy slugger." Stasha waved him down. "Just, turn

yourself off or something."

"You know I have no idea how to do that." Victor slumped back into his chair.

"Then go hang out with Arjie and find a way to simulate battle or something, I don't know!" Stasha was visibly stressed from the situation her bloodline got her into.

Victor thought about it. "That's not a bad idea, I'll go talk to him."

Serge stood up and took a closer look at the map. "Purmancia huh? I've only heard the stories. Nasty bit of people down there. Strange dialect too. Good entertainment though. Some of it can be..." He paused. "Weird."

"We'll have to make a pit stop or two for supplies but we should be fine for a while. The food storage is pretty well stocked." Kali closed the cabinet she was inspecting.

"Then it's settled." Stasha walked back into the cockpit and set a course. "Purmancia it is."

10

Victor leaned on the door frame to Sean's bunk-room. "So you can finally walk on your own again huh?"

Sean was lying on his back. The single, thick sheet he had was wrinkled with a restless sleep. He slowly sat himself upright and winced. "Baby steps lad. I can walk but I can't run."

"It's good to have you back, one way or another." Victor casually knocked on the door frame and waved goodbye as he turned around. He climbed down the access ladder to the cargo hold.

Victor skipped the last few rungs and landed with a metallic *thud*. He paused for a split second, somberly remembering his new weight. He turned to see Arjie sitting with his back to the wall. The massive humanoid war machine turned his head to greet Victor, and gave him a small wave.

"What have you been thinking about today ole' buddy?" Victor slapped the head of the ARJAC. A half comedic *tong* echoed briefly in the small space.

"Victor, I've been analyzing the geography of Purmancia and coming up with possible battle plans, in case we are tracked there." Arjie had put himself in low power mode since the long trip, but he still had full thought capabilities.

"Okay let's start from the beginning." Victor climbed over the railing, and onto Arjie's shoulder. One of his massive hands slowly rose and became a footrest for Victor.

"Purmancia is tidally locked, meaning that one side of the planet always faces its star." Arjie explained, "A thin, always sun-setting portion of the planet is habitable. The side facing the sun is an arid desert leading into a volcanic wasteland. The dark side of the planet is forever frozen over. The population is very dense in these areas in between. We have a better chance of blending in if we stay there."

"I've never been to a planet like that. How do they sleep?" Victor asked.

"According to my research, you get used to it. Most housing districts are on the darker side of the 'ring' while businesses and public areas are towards the lighter side."

"That's a pretty good way around a day-night routine when there isn't one to begin with," Victor observed.

"The two extremes of light and dark areas are used for either duels or ARJAC testing," Arjie went on. "Scrap piles are everywhere, either melting into the dusty ground, or freezing over in the frozen plains."

"Sounds like Grits would be all over this planet."

"Negative. Grits are usually not wealthy enough to own their own ARJAC. It is unsafe to go to either extreme without one, as you would die." Arjie warned.

"Lucky for us we have an ARJAC, and an android huh?" Victor sullenly stared at his metal feet.

"Correct," Arjie enthusiastically agreed. "We can possibly acquire enough salvaged parts to create one, or multiple ARJACs."

"That sounds like progress! Progress is very good right now," Victor said. "We have too many Steel Soldiers with only one ARJAC."

"Victor, I've also come up with hypothesized missions that might be offered once we register as mercenaries," Arjie continued.

"Oh?" Victor leaned forward slightly, "Do tell! Anything we can handle?"

"Affirmative. I suspect there will be leaders of gangs and other mercenary groups that have residence on Purmancia. Assassination missions will be a common occurrence here. Dueling arenas are also a way to make quick cash, as they are televised and bet on."

"So boxing, but in ARJAC's?" Victor asked.

"Correct."

"Sounds fun." Victor thought he heard excitement in Arjie's voice.

"It is very dangerous."

"And? That hasn't stopped us before," Victor retorted.

"We did not have a choice before," Arjie said flatly.

A silence filled the room, only broken by the occasional thumping of space debris against the hull and the whirring of mechanical processes.

Arjie finally broke the silence. "I would suggest taking part in an ARJAC duel once we are registered to show what we are capable of, then take on what we would consider an easy assassination mission. To successfully complete the assassination mission, we must keep your identity as a sentient android secret."

"I know what you're thinking of for the plan and I'm on board," Victor quickly agreed.

Stasha climbed down the ladder to greet Victor and Arjie. "How are my two favorite creations doing on this fine day?" The two turned simultaneously to acknowledge her, but quickly showed worry when the pilot was not at the helm. "Don't worry I have Serge watching over the controls." Stasha reassured them. "Arjie, how are you holding up down here? I know it can get lonely."

"I did this for twenty five years, I can do it for a couple months. Plus I don't have to watch Victor's vitals anymore... And I have a body." He clenched his fist in appreciation.

"That's... Good to hear I guess. Victor, how are you doing? Figure out how to eat yet?" Stasha teased.

"I'm so close to being able to do it on my own. I can get the visualization, but I can't get the manipulation part." Victor excitedly said.

"Progress is progress, keep at it you'll get it eventually." Stasha encouraged. "Also, we arrive tomorrow."

Victor nearly fell off of Arjie's shoulder. "Already? It's been that long?"

"Affirmative." Arjie responded.

"Okay so here's the plan, we don't split up, and I'll do the talking. Got it?" Stasha briefed Serge and Kali as the cargo bay door opened slowly. They both nodded. "First thing we need to do is register as a mercenary group. Victor and Arjie briefed me on their plan and I think it's a good one."

The bay doors collided with the wet tarmac. A bustling spaceport greeted them with indifference. No building was more than a few levels high on Purmancia except for the massive corporate buildings interrupting the horizon's eternal sunset. Flickering neon signs and ragged flags provided a canopy for the pedestrians. Vehicles of all sizes crowded the narrow roads, pushing people into the already densely packed sidewalks. The amount of people seeking what little fortune they could find on Purmancia left the general populace cold to anyone who wasn't immediately useful to them.

"Why are there so many signs?" Serge shielded his

eyes from the bright signs.

"Well, it's a gambling world where only ten percent can be lived in," Stasha clarified. "Okay let's see here." She read the signs out loud. "Tavern, casino, casino, ARJAC wash? Casino, hotel, casino, motel. Lotta casinos huh?" Stasha brushed herself off and mentally prepared herself for the amount of shoving she'd have to do.

"Well you did say it was a gambling world," Serge joked.

"Oh quiet you!" Kali retorted.

"Let's move you lovebirds, I don't want to be here all day." Stasha hurried down the ramp of the cargo door and kept scanning the signs. "Here we go! Public office! At the very least we can get directions."

The three proceeded through the crowded streets, the crowds only letting them into the flow after inspecting the entourage that approached. The small group of newcomers didn't dare go against the flow of foot traffic. They finally pushed their way to the revolving doors leading into the public office.

After waiting in line for a few hours, Stasha, Serge, and Kali eventually got to a teller. Her face was far too clean compared to what they had just roughed their way through. Her wrinkles were hidden behind what they could only guess was rejuvenate creams and genetics. "Hello, I just landed and was wondering where the mercenary creation offices were?" Stasha used her best polite voice.

The old woman behind the desk glanced up from her coffee and looked over the three standing before her. She sighed and slapped down a piece of paper and a clipboard.

The three sat down on surprisingly comfortable padded chairs. Stasha filled out the forms and stopped on the name of the group. "What do we call ourselves?" She looked to Serge and Kali for guidance.

"Damned if I know. I didn't make up any names." Serge flatly stated.

"I thought of baby names once, it was fun," Kali reminisced. "But not much else."

Stasha leaned back and stared at the ceiling. "Maybe something sentient? Because of Arjie, ya know? But what about Victor, he's there too, and you guys." She paused, lost in thought. "How about The Sentient Nightmare?"

Serge and Kali shook their heads.

"Right too edgy. You guys were all Nightcats so how about something like The Panthers?"

"That's totally taken already." Kali added.

"True, true." She clicked the pen on her chin. "How about The Demolition Proxy! Since they're all dead now."

"Didn't those guys kill your parents?" Serge asked.

Stasha paused for a moment, juggling the idea. "I'll put it down as a maybe."

After many more random ideas, the three decided to call the newly founded mercenary group "The Midnight Ocelot." Serge complained it was too cute of an animal, but Kali and Stasha outnumbered his vote.

Stasha gave the registration paper to the old desk lady along with a sum of money as a start-up fee. The three then headed towards the dueling arena betting houses. They stopped at the doors outside and Stasha turned to Serge.

"Serge I need you to be the biggest, burliest, most confident you can be. We need a big fight to get the peoples' heads turning. Can you do that?"

Without an answer, Serge immediately strode into the betting house. The dingy common room went quiet. Cigar smoke wafted and curled in the still air.

Serge stood proud and tall, "Alright which one of you faux-steel using wimps wants to fight my pilot?"

A well built man swaggered over to Serge and looked him over. They were practically nose to nose when they spoke to each other, unblinking.

"What ARJAC do you have, old man?" The brutish man mocked.

"Generation two weapons. S-ARJAC frame. Bantam-weight," Serge flatly replied.

"Think you can beat a Cruiser-weight with Gen-three weapons?"

"Now how'd you get those?" Serge jokingly asked.

"You scared?" The man pushed his nose even closer.

"Never." Serge held his ground. He was a coiled viper ready to strike at any provocation.

The brutish man turned around and gathered the looks from his associates. His pilot swiveled around on a bar stool. Her hair was shaved to the scalp. A wrinkled and stained jumpsuit barely covered a body covered in a mess of scars and tattoos. She scoffed at Serge and went back to drinking.

"My pilot thinks you're in the wrong place, old man."

"How about this?" Serge suggested, "We fight. Right now. First to-"

The brutish man swung a suckerpunch straight to Serge's jaw. Serge deftly dodged the attack, grabbed his arm, and broke it over his knee. The brutish man screamed in agony as Serge walked out the door.

"I'll see you in two days to fight. Your pilot better be sober." Serge spat on the floor as he walked out the doors.

Two uneventful days passed. The crew worked slowly to check over Arjie and his components. When the time finally came for Victor's duel, the mood shifted to a buzz of excitement.

Victor climbed into his ARJAC and started the systems check.

Engine: Online. Sensory cameras: Online. Joint rotation: Online. Oxygen supply: not important. Radar Pulse: Online.

A low bass filled the cockpit and reverberated the surrounding loading chamber.

Helmet integration is not needed anymore Victor you can stop flipping the switch. You're already plugged in so I'll transfer your view to be the ARJAC's.

"Sorry Arjie it's a habit at this point, and it's not a bad habit so let me be." Victor sat back in the cockpit, tensing and releasing his manufactured hand.

Good thing you're not a perfectionist.

Serge's voice crackled over the radio, "This duel is televised on the local stations so look pretty for the cameras. You'll hear the announcer start to hype up the crowds in a few moments. Go get 'er Victor."

"Hey Arjie," Victor inquired. "What tricks do we have up our sleeve?"

Besides the huge advantage of having me, nothing. Too hot for cloak tech, no fancy maneuvering abilities. Just the AMC-2 and the rotary machine gun on your back. Well and a knife.

"Do we know what the other pilot has?"

Not a clue. I believe that's the rules around here. No public information about your opponent or their ARJAC. You get to salvage whatever you want from the loser though, which is pretty neat.

"Let's hope she has something we don't have then." Victor was getting excited. It had been months since he had piloted Arjie.

An over-the-top announcer's voice echoed through the cylindrical loading elevator, "Look alive pilots! We have a newcomer challenging our regional bruiser today! Fresh off of the shuttle, we have the challenging team, the Midnight Ocelots! No pilot names were given so we're sticking with that! The defender is none other than Amelia Portar!"

"I take it she's good then?" Victor asked.

Judging by the slight nuances in the announcer's voice, she is locally a champion but not the best on the planet.

The platform jerked and started slowly rising upwards. A hatch opened above Victor, letting in sunlight.

"Looks like it's time to win then." He steeled his nerves for the fight.

Victor rose up and was hit with a wave of dust. Sand slowly poured into the elevator shaft.

It appears to be roughly ninety degrees Celsius here Victor. You will be fine if you step outside but it is not recommended for long periods. If you wish to keep your circuits running smoothly I suggest winning.

"Thanks for the heads up. So where's Amelia?" Victor was scanning the shimmering horizon in front of him.

Visual scans indicate that she is out of sight, but directly ahead of you. That's how these things tend to work. I suggest finding some cover.

"Arjie, do you think my left arm can integrate with anything or is it just specific guns?" Victor asked.

Just guns.

"Well there goes that plan," Victor said solemnly. He wanted a shield.

Victor jumped back and crouched behind the massive hatch that had flipped open. He peeked out, with the rotary machine gun in the ready position.

I recommend short bursts. Your weapons will overheat quickly in this heat.

"Thanks for the tip." Victor scanned the horizon over and over, waiting to see movement. The announcer's voice echoed below him in the lift. The words were unrecognizable. A small amount of sand slipped downwards from a nearby dune.

Movement, eleven o'clock.

"I see it. But is it her?" Victor focused on the area for a few moments. No more movement.

A shot rang out and tore through the hatch Victor was hiding behind. "Where the hell did that come from?" he shouted in surprise.

Judging by the exit hole, and how it did not damage us, I would say it came from roughly two o'clock, with the same distance as the movement at eleven.

"Does she have a PASS?" Victor did a sweeping spray from his machine gun.

Too early to say, we were focusing on a different area. I recommend a slight retreat. I will watch behind as best I can.

Victor dashed to the nearest dune, hurling himself behind it and digging into the sand. Another shot thudded into the desert where he just was.

Good news Victor, no stealth tech on this one. Only a perfectly crafted covering that blends into the sand with no way of telling the difference. Also the shot fired was rather low for what Serge said was a cruiser weight class ARJAC. This may be a custom model I am unfamiliar with.

"Couldn't it just be laying down?"

That is a possibility.

"So what's the plan here? I thought we were supposed to put on a show."

Victor quickly looked over the dune and a glint showed through the blazing sun. "I found her." He braced his AMC-2 in the sand and let out a shot. The sand vibrated with the power of the shot and fell away from the canon. The shot landed on target with a grating metal-on-metal *boom*. The shockwave of the impact sent out a ripple of sand in all directions.

Shot on target, judging from the impact she must have an external shield.

"Wait like a fancy shield generator from the movies?"

No, a metal wall. Shield generators don't exist.

"Oh, right. That means she's a stationary sniper type, right? We can use this."

You'll have to be quick, she can easily just pick up the shield and move it.

"I know. I have a plan to counteract that. If she's a sniper, the last thing she'd want is for me to get in close. But to close the gap... she wants me to do that." Victor was given countless hours of anti-sniper training thanks to Kali being on the Nightcat team.

I know the conundrum. They call it the Target's Enigma. We should probably do that plan of yours and not just chat.

"Oh yeah. Sorry it's been a bit since I've been in a fight. I guess I was having a bit too much fun." Victor broke through the dune, kicking up sand and causing a makeshift smokescreen. He sprinted towards Amelia's last location, running in a serpentine pattern and collecting more sand as he went. Each time the dust cleared he threw another handful and picked up more, repeating the process several times.

Shots skimmed past Victor, causing dents and scrapes but no major damage. Victor leaped over the dune where Amelia was shooting from. He landed and turned around. Nothing was there.

"Wasn't she supposed to be right here?" Victor frantically looked around.

I tracked her shots to this spot. She must have experience with people rushing her.

A hand breached through the sand and grabbed Victor's leg. The camouflaged covering flew away to reveal an ARJAC half-buried in the sand. The thick armor slightly vibrated to dispel the sand for ease of entry into the desert.

Now that's a cool feature.

"Shut up, we're losing." Victor's mind was racing, trying to think of a way out of the ARJAC's grip.

Use your knife dumbass.

Victor grabbed the knife on his hip and cut a deep gash in the arm holding him in place, attempting to drag him into the sand. Amelia was forced to let go. Victor grabbed the dual shoulder mounted AMC-3P's on her ARJAC and crushed the barrels.

Amelia dug herself out of the hole and engaged in a weak display of melee combat. She swung wide, and Victor used her momentum to trip her. She fell into the sand face first. Victor put his foot on her back, which would only give him a slight time advantage. Her ARJAC's power output was far greater than his.

She pushed her ARJAC to the breaking point as she attempted to stand with Arjie's full weight on her back. Sparks and oil burst from the joints. Everything was being put into trying to win at this exact moment, but she just couldn't stand after all the damage she had taken.

Victor put a round of the AMC-2 into the back of Amelia's ARJAC and it stopped struggling. She wasn't dead, but she was beaten. Horns and sirens blazed, echoing through the barren desert. A small drone came down from the sky and displayed a holographic winner's card. The announcer's annoying voice came from the drone.

"We have a HUGE upset here folks! The desert queen is defeated! I bet everyone watching sure feels jealous of this new team!"

Serge's voice reappeared in Victor's radio. "Victor, I'm being told you need to go to the hatch that brought you up, also we're taking that ARJAC back. Kali will love it. I saw the look in her eyes when it first appeared on screen."

Victor made his way to the hatch. Serge's voice interrupted the good mood of the moment. "Also they're asking for an interview. Well, demanding. Can't get outta this one."

Victor arrived at the bottom of the massive lift and was greeted with news crews and new fans. Victor disconnected and took a robotic deep breath. He opened the hatch and stepped out into public view. The crowd fell silent. He could see the red lights of recording cameras pointed at him.

"I really don't like this." Victor waved sheepishly at the silent crowd. He was being as robotic as he could be in the mentally weary state he was in.

They erupted in a massive applause.

"This can't be good for our secrecy," he mumbled to himself.

He climbed down and turned to face the reporters. They were a sea of bodies and voices.

"Who programmed you? Are you a factory model? I haven't seen your type. Why are you wearing clothes? Where'd you get that jacket?" The questions didn't stop and there was no way for Victor to focus on one.

"I'm uhhh. Not a robot. I'm a human. Well, my consciousness is," Victor nervously said.

"That's impossible, technology hasn't gone that far yet. Who programmed you? What planet were you made on?" the reporters badgered Victor.

"Ummm Earth? That's where this body came from at least."

"You're from EARTH?" The reporters had the scoop of their lifetime.

"Y-yeah," he stammered. Victor was getting more and more uncomfortable with the obsessive reporters.

Serge pushed his way through the crowd and blocked Victor from the reporters. "Hey if you people want to answer questions, how about you ask the *human*? Let my pilot get some maintenance!"

Victor was begrudgingly let through the crowd while Serge started answering questions from the reporters.

"I don't like being famous."

"So we didn't make all that much money with that fight." Stasha looked over the newly acquired ARJAC, "Fine piece of machinery though I'll give you that. Victor, you did a good job on keeping it intact."

Victor shrugged. "It was just the most efficient way I could win. Robots think in numbers after all."

Stasha shook her head. "Victor don't get all broody just because strangers think you're a robot! You have to have a clear head to win against these people. They don't play fair."

"I can win with one hand. Everyone underestimates androids, they aren't built to kill most of the time. We can use it to our advantage." Victor sat on an ammunition crate. "So what's the next step here? We can't stay much longer. Not with my fight being broadcasted to the entire galaxy."

"It may have been recorded live, but the story about you being made of gears and gizmos isn't until 'tonight'." Serge said as he walked into the makeshift repair bay. "Also, Victor you have another fight coming up tomorrow. This time they came to ME. Felt like the old days if even for a little bit."

"Who is it this time?" Victor flatly asked.

"Pilot by the name of Emile Pirtuois. Came up to me himself, weird accent though it took me a second to figure out what he was saying."

"Do we know the specs on his ARJAC?" Victor leaned forward, his mind in business mode.

"From what I gathered on the reruns, he pilots a Flyweight ARJAC with a PASS, so it's hard to tell much else," Stasha added.

"Stealth huh?" Victor stroked his chin. "Do we know where the fight will happen? Preferably we'd want the desert again for the immense heat the PASS generates."

"That would be ideal, yes. I've heard Emile has some pull in the fighting ring though, something about being from a big family. He could talk to the organizers for a fight in the colder regions," Serge said.

"I don't know if I'll be able to deal with him if it's in the snow. The PASS is something that very few can effectively counter," Victor thought out loud.

"Well then let's hope the organizers still underestimate you and want to see a good fight rather than a stomping." Serge started to walk back to the reporters and turned around at the doorway. "Good luck kid."

Looks like we have a chance.

The somehow familiar desert elevator tube boomed with the annoying announcer's voice again.

"Look alive pilots! We have another great fight today! We have the Robot of Rumbles versus Emile Pirtuois! Can The Midnight Ocelot team take him on? Or will Emile use that special skill of his to stomp this newcomer into the ground? Let's fiiiiiiind out!"

The elevator started to rise. The hatch above Victor opened, letting in a dusty whirlwind. These kinds of geological events were already too familiar to Victor. His memory and adaptability was getting better.

It appears a storm of some kind is starting. At long distances his PASS will be super effective, but at closer ranges it will essentially be null. The sand will stick to the ARJAC making an outline.

"I'll take any chance I get. Do we know what weapons he uses?" Victor checked the systems again to make sure everything was running smoothly.

Judging from wind speeds, no matter what weapon is used, it will severely veer off course. Close combat is advised.

"That sounds like a good thing for us then." Victor closed his eyes and leaned his head back for a moment. The lift reached the top and the winds almost blew Victor over. "Arjie, can you adjust for the winds?"

I will do my best.

Victor braced himself against the wind and started a defensive sweep. "There's no point running around looking for him. He'll just avoid me. I'll have to be the mouse in this scenario." He didn't like being hunted. If Victor could, he'd be close to nausea from nerves.

Scanning for tremors will be hard in the sand as well. I will try to call out activity as I see it.

"Thanks Arjie, I doubt I can do it alone." It was comforting to have Arjie inside his head this time.

Footprints ten o'clock!

Victor sprayed a line of machine gun rounds in the general direction. A couple rounds hit their mark, sparking the air. Emile shot a Gauss Rifle round at Victor, skimming off of his shoulder.

Victor spun in place, searching for the next emergence of Emile. A minute that seemed like hours went by of nothing but the wind tearing through the desert. A swift kick in the back left Victor staggering. Another Gauss Rifle round pierced Victor's ankle, severely hindering his movement.

"This can't be good." Victor struggled to return fire, missing his shots.

Emile faded back into the sandstorm. Moments later he sprang out, tackling Victor to the ground. He tore a hole through Victor's right arm, rending it. The arm flopped about as Victor spun, looking for Emile's ARJAC. It banged against his legs and chest.

We have lost AMC-2 capabilities.

Emile leapt away. Almost immediately, Emile shot a point blank Gauss Rifle round into Victor's hip. Victor did not even have time to notice he was behind him before Emile stealthily vanished again.

Victor, I believe we will win this. If my projections are accurate that is.

"How are we going to win? I can barely stand, let alone fight!" Victor wasn't used to losing real battles.

Just survive the next hit.

"I don't know, maybe I'll just try to-" Victor was cut off as Emile took his legs out from under him. Victor hit the ground hard. "That would've knocked me unconscious."

Emile raised his Gauss Rifle, targeting the cockpit of Victor's ARJAC. Victor couldn't even struggle, he was perfectly pinned. Victor stared down the barrel of his death, but it never came.

"Just shoot me already!" Victor shouted. "I'm tired of waiting!"

Emile's ARJAC has overheated and emergency shutdowns were initiated.

"I can't move to win though. How the hell are we supposed to get out of this?" Victor asked angrily. "Is it going to be a stalemate?"

Do they allow ties?

"We can't settle for a tie, we need that PASS." Victor regained some lost hope.

Then you will have to disembark.

"What? How am I supposed to win against an

ARJAC with nothing but a holdout pistol?" Victor tried to think of another way, struggling to break free from the inoperable ARJAC.

You must climb Emile's ARJAC and open the hatch.

"That sounds like a terrible plan. Won't I die in this heat?" Victor searched for his pistol as he spoke.

Negative. Your body is made of a material that has a high melting point. Very good for situations like this.

Victor disconnected from Arjie and opened the cockpit hatch. "Wish me luck I guess." He caught himself right before the hatch fully let in the desert. He had been moving subconsciously, as if he already knew he would be fine.

The wind knocked his head forward. Victor zipped up his jacket and headed towards one of Emile's legs. The sand scratched against him with a loud metallic tearing. He looked up at the ARJAC and shook his head. "I'm going to have sand in my body for weeks after this. Sorry Stasha."

He began to climb. A television periscope emerged beside him, following his every move. "I guess the drones can't handle the weather."

The wind threw one of Victor's hands as he reached the waist of the ARJAC. He held on as best he could, waiting for a slight dip in the fierceness of the wind. He managed to get both of his hands back onto the ARJAC and continued to the hatch. The wind deafened any other noise Victor might have heard. He did a few test shouts, but they were lost to the wind.

Victor fiddled with the override hatch to open the cockpit. "He can't survive long in this heat. I just have to tell him that and he'll concede right? I hope he doesn't have a gun either. Though I guess it is likely that he does." Victor continued to mutter to himself before finally opening the hatch."

Emile was waiting with a pistol pointed at the hatch. He shakily shot his entire magazine at Victor. A round tore through his left forearm and thigh. The other ten rounds grazed off of Victor or missed completely.

Victor stood his ground, with his pistol pointed at Emile. His silhouette looming over the panicking pilot. "Reload and I shoot. If you make this hard for you, you WILL die." Victor shouted over the wind. It was slightly quieter in Emile's cockpit compared to the outside.

Emile threw his gun to the feet of Victor and silently raised his hands. Victor took the gun and closed the hatch, keeping the unbearable heat outside of Emile's cockpit.

Victor jumped into the sand, falling onto his back. He sat up and raised his hand, giving a thumbs up. "I win."

A few minutes later a recovery team was on site, in protective gear. They loaded Victor and the two ARJACs into transport trucks, fitted with caterpillar treads. Victor slumped in the backseat as the two workers excitedly talked about the fight.

The trucks reached an elevator hatch, the workers

radioed down to open the hatch, and a few seconds later they were on the elevator down to the safety of the underground tunnels.

Serge was already answering the reporters' questions when Victor got out of the truck without any help. He was limping his way over to the rental car Serge used but was stopped by reporters for a picture. Victor weakly stood still as reporters got pictures from all angles while asking questions about the fight.

"I just want to get fixed up, this hurts you know," Victor lied. He couldn't feel anything.

Serge pushed the reporters back and helped Victor into the car. "You're becoming quite popular around here kid! Everyone wants you to work for them now. I think duels are out of the question for a while though. You took a beating. Let's get you fixed up. I already have another job for us. It'll involve the PASS we got today and the new ARJAC. This one should be the last one before we have to shove off, the Prol definitely know we're here now."

Victor looked at the cameras and back to Serge. "I don't think I'll miss it here."

11

"So what's this 'last job' that you're talking about?" Victor sat with Sean and Kali while Serge stood next to a hand drawn map. They were all crowded in the small meeting room on Stasha's ship.

"We just have to kill a government official," Serge said jovially.

"Why the hell are we doing this?" Kali asked. She crossed her arms.

"This seems a little high brow for a group that's only been on the planet for two weeks." Sean agreed.

Serge turned back to his drawing, ignoring the small audience. "The fact that we are leaving is why this group hired us. Obviously I don't know the name of the group, but they are a rebel faction attempting to stage a coup. Apparently the prime minister here is a very corrupt man. They didn't tell me much else besides the bare minimum. Location, target details, vague motive. The meeting was something out of a spy movie." Serge smiled.

"So what is their plan once we do this? Are they going to do a radical change in government or just elect a new prime minister?" Victor asked. He wasn't all that curious but asked as a formality.

"I don't know one way or another, but we have a very high paying job which will keep us set for a long time," Serge said. "I'll go over the details now, so pay attention."

Serge drew a circle where there was a flat area in the topographical map. "This is where our target lives. It's a remote house pretty deep into the colder hemisphere. There are guards, all of them heavily armed. We cannot bring an ARJAC so you have to go on foot. Victor and Kali will be going. Sean, you still need to rest."

Sean sighed and leaned back. He wasn't going to complain.

"This is where I will drop you off." Serge drew a square quite a distance away from the circle marking where the house was. "The public roads end there, it's the closest I can get you without arousing suspicion."

"If you drew this map right, that's at least a four hour hike through subzero temperatures with only minimal light. I know I can make it, but will Kali?" Victor observed flatly.

"I'll be fine, I've been bulking up," Kali jested. She flexed one of her muscular arms.

Victor looked her over. "You look the same to me."

"That's because you don't know the ins and outs of a woman's body." Kali laughed.

"I barely know the ins and outs of my own body,"

Victor said flatly.

"So, what are they bringin'?" Sean asked, diverting back to the subject.

"Right." Serge refocused. "Victor will be bringing a pair of high zoom binoculars and a PDW, Kali will be bringing a sniper rifle and some nice high explosive rounds. And some AP rounds just in case." Serge picked up a box from behind a door. He dropped it in front of Victor, Sean, and Kali. It landed with a monotone thud.

They opened it and pulled out two white pieces of cloth.

"Fresh bed sheets?" Sean asked.

"No, they're old-fashioned warmth and camouflage mixed into one conveniently priced package." Serge smiled. "Just don't rely on it by wearing a t-shirt underneath. Victor, you need this mainly so that you don't shine like a beacon."

"Fair enough." Victor spoke as he inspected his polished arm.

"Now get ready, you two. The raid is tonight. Any questions?"

Victor raised his hand, "What will the target be doing when we arrive at the objective?"

"They told me he should be getting ready to host a party," Serge replied. "Shame I couldn't be there to see it. I hear Purmancian parties are lavish, at least the rich ones."

Serge pointed to a picture of a middle aged looking man with greasy black hair. "This is the prime minister and our target. I can't give you a picture because if we're caught before we get there the operation is over before it even starts. Any more questions?"

The three shook their heads.

"Then let's get going."

The eternally sun-setting sky shone a deep, pale yellow. Kali and Victor trudged through the deep snow. The snow-capped evergreen trees dotted the hillside. No animal tracks could be seen anywhere the two looked. The harsh subzero temperatures limited Kali's concentration. Even for her countless hours of training, sometimes it just wasn't enough for mother nature.

"We need to take a new route with less snow on the way back, I bet there will be people scrambling to find us once we pull the trigger," Kali noted. "We'll be too easy to track in this snow." She looked back at the nearly foot deep tracks they made.

Faint lights shimmered on the snow like a mirror, shifting colors from blue to yellow, red, green, purple, orange and everything in between.

"We're getting close." Victor noticed as he stomped through the iced-over snow.

"How are you holding up Victor? Is anywhere seizing up? Did Stasha repair you up nice and proper?"

Kali asked, trying to get her mind off of the cold.

"Speak for yourself Kali, I can hear your teeth chattering from all the way over here." Victor laughed without mirth.

A gust of warm air whipped his makeshift cloak. He swatted it downwards so that he could see again.

"Warm air?" Kali paused. "Is he using heating generators just to have a warmer outside?" She welcomed the change in temperature.

"Well Serge did say there was a party tonight." Victor continued onward, crouching lower when he could. "Maybe they're grilling some exotic foods. Can't have the fumes and smoke inside." He knew that wasn't the reason for the heat.

Another blast of warm air enveloped the shivering sniper and the unnerved android. The pulsing lights almost blinded them as they came to the top of the final hill. The two crouched in the snow, pulling the cloaks over them, looking like snow-covered rocks.

"Just how much energy is being used to heat this place? I'm practically sweating here." Kali shook her cloak to temporarily improve airflow.

Victor pulled out his binoculars and scanned the estate. He saw green grass behind a massive wall. There were heating generators lining the wall, with snow guards on the tops. The estate was massive, almost as big as Stasha's workshop. Guests emerged from their cars wearing little more than what was necessary to cover the essentials. Following each of the scantily clad, giddily laughing guests were one or two drably dressed people. They shuffled after their designated guest, and seemed to be put into some kind of pain and hurried to catch up if they strayed too far. Guests exchanged remotes of some kind. The servants followed whomever was holding their remote. Servants exiting the estate and getting back into cars with the leaving guests seemed excited.

"Kali, do you see this?" Victor hadn't seen anything like it before.

"Where's the Prime Minister though? He's not greeting the guests." Kali looked through her scope. She scanned each quadrant of the bustling estate.

"Why do you think they're dressed like that? Is it just that hot? Are those other people servants?" Victor continued looking through his binoculars. "The servants seem to look dejected. I think they aren't being treated right."

"I don't think it's a regular party, Victor. Look closer." Kali's voice darkened tremendously.

An attendant checked in the guests, and scanned their "servants." Moments later the group would go inside. Victor watched a group check in and go inside. The group then made their way past some guests standing and chatting. They grabbed what looked like a truncheon.

"They grabbed a truncheon, and maybe a taser?" Victor observed inquisitively.

"That's not a taser, or a truncheon." Kali's mood

worsened further.

"Then what are they? Oh." Victor fell silent.

"I've heard of these things existing. I never thought I'd see one for myself," Kali said darkly. "Damn this planet's government."

Victor dropped his binoculars. "I think I need a minute."

"I think we need to sit tight for a while and think up a plan anyway. I'm not seeing the target anywhere." Kali continued to scan the estate. "He must be inside. Maybe he knows we're after him?"

"Clearly, this can't be accepted culturally." Victor brought himself back to a functioning state of mind. "He knows it's dangerous to be outside with this kind of stuff going down." He put the binoculars to his eyes again. "Do you see if there's an unusually high concentration of guards?"

"I'm seeing something on the far end, past the queue of cars." Kali focused on the area. "There are guards in front of what looks like a glorified tool shed."

Victor stood up. "I'll head over there and take a look."

"We'd have to loop around in order to get any clearer of a picture or a shot, let's save that for after we've completely used this angle." Kali was trying to settle Victor's nerves.

"Roger." He crouched back down.

Kali continued to scan the estate. "I see some shadows through the tinted windows in what looks like an offshoot from a main hallway. Quite a few actually."

"I take it I don't want to know?" Victor wasn't looking through his binoculars anymore.

"Yup." Kali said flatly.

"I'll keep looking around the perimeter, you focus on the estate." He stood up again.

"Hey Victor?"

"Yeah?" Victor looked back at Kali.

"Can you change your range of visible lights?" she asked.

Victor stopped and thought for a moment. "Maybe a little. Let me try." He turned and stared at the estate for a minute. "I don't see why I wouldn't be able to. I've been able to train a lot these days with Arjie, so it's possible that I can do it by myself."

He saw silhouettes vaguely resembling humans pressed together. Some were still, some were moving quickly. He quickly turned around and shook his head. "I can, and I know where the target is. You're not going to like what I have in mind though."

"I take it there's a problem?" Kali asked.

"Yup. The target is in a centralized chamber. By the way the glass bends light, it appears to be thick and bullet proof," Victor explained. "He's surrounded by both guards and guests. and innocents."

"Let me guess." Kali groaned.

"I think we have to go in."

"So do you even have a plan?" Kali asked.

"Well I have a vague idea, so I guess it's better than usual," Victor thought out loud. "Luckily I don't think you'll need to wear those skimpy outfits everyone else is wearing."

"Well that's a plus," Kali joked flatly.

"Yeah, you'll need to smuggle weapons in," Victor elaborated. "And you definitely can't do that wearing nothing."

"So what's the PLAN Victor?" Kali grew impatient, she didn't like the idea of rubbing elbows with these people.

"Okay, okay, here it goes." Victor took a synthetic deep breath and explained. "So see that shack on the far side? With the amount of guards there, there has to be. uhm... Party goers."

"Right. So?"

"We get into that shack undetected, you take the clothes of the servant, I'll take whatever tools that are there." Victor struggled to think of the tactful words for the situation.

"Won't that make you the owner of me?" She stared

at him with suspicious eyes.

"Not exactly. I'll pretend to be just a servant android, while you be my owner. There's bound to be someone like that on this crazy planet, right?"

"Well I guess it's possible," Kali thought. "I don't like the idea of being treated like some object."

"Yeah I don't either," Victor agreed. "So let's get in, kill him quick, and get out before anyone catches on."

Kali stood up and started trudging towards the other side of the estate. "Let's get a move on then, Victor. I don't want to be stuck between sweating and shivering forever."

Victor followed her until they reached the shack. The air was considerably warmer, and the ground was wet with melting snow.

"How many guards?" Victor hid behind a tree, attempting to dry himself off so that he would not glisten.

"Let's see." Kali counted under her breath. "It looks like maybe four or five within visible range of the shack. We only need to take care of maybe two in order to actually get in though."

"I have a plan to draw them out, be ready." Victor prepared himself.

"Wait, what are you doing Victor?" Kali tried to stop him without raising her voice too loudly.

Victor fell off the high wall and plummeted into the soggy grass next to the shack. He landed face down. Two guards saw Victor land and hurried over to see the commotion. Victor mechanically brought himself to his feet and looked at the guards.

"Location unknown. Please tell me where I am so that I may go to my master." Victor spoke in a monotone, mimicking an android. His face was covered in mud. Kali had to stifle a laugh.

The two guards looked at each with confused faces. Kali dropped from above and pounced onto one of the guards, quickly snapping his neck. Victor grabbed the other guard's head and quickly cracked his skull between his palms. He kept the pressure until he heard the sharp sound of bone breaking. The two silently dragged the bodies to a dark corner. Kali draped the two makeshift camouflage cloaks over them, attempting to mimic a pile of snow. Luckily, their injuries were all internal.

"When did you get so strong?" Kali asked as she brushed Victor off.

"Well to be honest, I don't know. Just kind of felt like I could do that one day," Victor nonchalantly answered. "I surprised myself a little bit with how effective that was."

"Well okay then strongman, give me a boost then." Kali pointed to a small rectangular window.

Victor helped her up. When Kali climbed in, there was a quick yelp followed by a scuffle. Kali moved some furniture to stand on to help Victor through. Victor climbed effortlessly through the window.

"Who's the strong one here?" Victor jokingly asked, "I weigh more than a Gauss Rifle round."

"Yeah, well you're not the only one with robotic strength," Kali assured him.

"Is there supposed to be this much blood?" Victor asked as he scanned the interior of the shack.

"Well, I may have made a little more." Kali motioned to the corpse of what was most likely an aristocrat with some kind of giant screw coming out of their stomach. "I wish they didn't put up a fight. It didn't have to end like this for them."

"I think they might have deserved it." Victor nodded towards a table in the middle of the shack. A naked corpse covered in restraining harnesses lay on a table, limbs bound to the corners. A giant drill press sparkled red above the lifeless subject.

"These poor people. No one deserves this much suffering," Kali lamented.

"I would be sick if I could feel any sort of bodily function. Let's just get out of here," Victor urged.

Kali picked up the clothing that lay thrown in a corner. She hid a pistol in each of her boots, with Victor's small PDW strapped to her back, covered by a rough tunic.

Kali took a deep breath. "So where to?"

"Directly to the center of the estate, once we enter head upstairs. There's a giant glass overlook. That's where I saw him." Victor grabbed a whip and wrapped it on his shoulder. "Just in case, have to make it believable."

The two walked out of the shack and rounded a corner towards the main building. Two guards noticed them walking by and quizzically looked at them. One shook his head and scoffed at the whole idea of the party he was guarding.

"At least not everyone likes the idea of this," Victor quietly said.

Kali and Victor were stopped by a guard at the main entrance. "Where's your master, *dreg*? I can get you a master REAL quick."

"Oh no I'm not one of those rabble," Kali quickly corrected him with a commanding tone. "Here's my invite."

The guard snatched the piece of paper out of Kali's hand and looked it over. His face turned red. "My apologies Ms. Langly! I had no idea it was you."

"It's alright, I can see the confusion. DON'T let it happen again though!" Kali reprimanded the guard and pushed past him into the main building.

"That was some good thinking back there, how did you know they had an invite?" Victor asked.

"Well with something like this, there's always an invite, you can't just let anyone in." Kali tucked the paper back into her rough clothing.

She started climbing the stairs, stopped to survey the estate, where the guards were, and if there were any security cameras, just in case a quick escape was needed. Victor shoved her.

"MOVE" he commanded, then in a softer voice, "Sorry, have to make it more believable."

Stuck up business people and politicians wearing the bare minimum of clothing leered at Kali. She continued to climb the elaborate staircase while trying to avoid eye contact with any of the high class people. They reached the glass box suspended in the center of the estate. Kali tried to open the door, but it was locked.

"Victor, is he still in there?" she asked quietly.

Victor quickly fixed his gaze on the door, then shook his head to try to forget the image. "He's still there."

"Okay. Be ready." Kali nodded at Victor. She kicked down the door, breaking the locking mechanism.

"What the hell is going on here? Who are you? Where are your masters?" the Prime Minister shouted.

Kali quickly grabbed a pistol from her boot and shot him. The chubby man slumped over, then fell off of the enormous bed he was sitting on. A pool of blood started to form at the foot of the bed. The guards within the room drew their rifles, but Kali quickly shot them both through the forehead before they could fire a single round. Their heads' contents exploded onto the walls behind them as they dropped like dolls.

The other "masters" in the room started to panic. The servants saw the opportunity and bludgeoned them to death with whatever they could find. The corpses were not left in one piece.

"Victor!" Kali shouted.

Victor quickly wrapped the whip around the two doorknobs, barricading the group into the room. The servants looked at Kali. She had inadvertently become the leader of a revolt.

"Guards definitely heard those shots, they'll be coming any second. The whip will only give us a minute or two. We need to come up with a good plan." She tossed Victor his PDW. She looked at the three servants. "Anyone know how to shoot?"

One shakily raised her hand. "My dad taught me how when I was younger."

"Good enough." Kali tossed Victor's pistol to her.

The servant inspected it with trembling hands. "This is different from anything I've shot."

"Safety is on the right, the rest is the same." Kali loaded her spare magazine. She put the half used one back in her boot. "Shout if you're out. You have ten rounds. I have a spare six."

The servant nodded.

Guards shouted outside. They tried to open the

door. It opened slightly and Victor punched a guard in the face, shattering his forehead with a dull crack. Victor quickly jumped to the side, avoiding a spray of retaliation gunfire.

"Victor, can you break this glass?" Kali asked calmly.

"I can try, it's pretty thick." Victor made his way to the left wall of thick, tinted glass. He punched the solid glass, and a slight crack formed.

"Keep at it soldierman, but be quick," Kali encouraged. A spark of urgency sliced the words.

Victor punched again. A web of fractures cracked into existence. He kicked the glass, causing a bigger web of fractures to appear. He wound back and punched the glass one more time, shattering half of the wall. Everyone on the bottom level fell silent and looked up.

Kali appeared in the hole left behind by Victor and shouted, "The Prime Minister is dead! If you want your masters to join him in hell, now is the time! You should not be treated like this! Take back your lives! Purmancia should not have to live in fear of the corrupt! Take. back. PURMANCIA!"

"So how are we getting out of this one Kali?" Victor turned his attention away from the door. "They'll be through any second now."

Gunfire sporadically broke through the shouting and bludgeoning of bureaucrats. "Well hopefully we won't have to do much." Kali watched the carnage unfold beneath her. "I wonder how long these people were treated like this."

"For me, it's been a few years," One of the servants in the room meekly spoke. "I think."

"I haven't seen my kids in five years."

"I miss my parents."

"My kids should be just about done with school now. I hope they're doing alright."

The door burst open to the chamber the group was barricaded in. A pile of struggling bodies landed at Victor's feet. Guards were getting beaten by servants, some of them were long since dead.

The servants looked up from their obsessive beating and saw Kali. They stood, nodded, and turned around, searching for more people to satiate their lust for revenge. They made it to the bottom of the stairs before two guards mowed them down with their rifles. Their bodies fell in a heap, blood pooling around them.

"We better get going before reinforcements show up. We're already outnumbered as it is." Victor peered down the stairs from behind one of the doors. He shot a single round, piercing a guard's helmet. A unique metallic pang sounded as the guard crumpled and landed hard on the polished floor.

"You guys stay behind us." Kali started giving orders. "What's your name?" She motioned to the girl holding Victor's pistol.

"I-I'm Nadia." She seemed to gain confidence in

telling someone her name. She looked surprised she remembered her own name.

"Nadia, you stay behind the group. You'll be our rear guard. Don't let anyone sneak up behind us okay?" Kali's tone was calming and practiced.

"I'll do my best!" Her eyes lit up. "You can count on me."

Kali stood before the doorway, "Okay everyone! We're getting out of here! Stay behind us and don't stray far. We'll be out of here in maybe five minutes."

The small group murmured and shuffled into a staggered line. Victor gave the all-clear signal to Kali and they started to descend the grand stairs. On either side, servants and guards fought. Bodies of both sides were littered among the fights.

"The main entrance is a bad idea, let's loop to the back, probably less guards there. Also the police will get there last, which gives us a little bit of extra time," Victor explained as he scanned for guards who weren't caught up in fights.

The group skirted along the base of the stairs until they reached the dining hall. Guards were shouting inside. Victor stood on one side of the doorway with Kali on the other. He motioned for the group to stand against the wall, away from the door. Victor quickly stood in the doorway and sprayed half of his PDW magazine into the group. It fired so fast it sounded like the loudest bug in existence. The guards fell, their bodies being torn apart by the small caliber rounds. Victor quickly poked his head into the room and scanned for any more guards.

"Clear." He said as he passed through the doorway, motioning for the rest to follow.

A massive table took up most of the room. Chairs that originally lined the table were scattered and broken. A guard was lying in the center of the table, crucified using kitchen knives and a sharpened chair leg. Blood dripped from the table in a perfectly uniform manner. A bloodied knife was lodged into the table next to his throat.

"What a creative bunch," Victor jested as they passed the body.

"I wish I could've been there. I remember this guard from the last couple years," Nadia stated. "One of the worst ones, loved to participate."

Kali shuddered. "Okay, let's just find the kitchen. There's usually a door to the outside in there."

"Looks like it's this way!" Victor peered around the corner into a tiled kitchen. Multiple sinks, stove-tops, and ovens were neatly arranged next to the preparation tables.

The group made their way into the kitchen. When Nadia was just about to pass through the doorway, a guard entered the dining hall. He saw the servants escaping and quickly sprayed a burst at them. Nadia was shot in her leg. She yelped and staggered, bracing herself against the wall. She quickly returned fire, shooting the guard twice. She limped to a safer spot that was easier for her to lean on her good leg.

Kali quickly turned and attempted to help Nadia. Nadia locked eyes with Kali and showed a stern, determined look. She recognized those eyes and Kali understood immediately that if the group tried to help Nadia escape, their chances of survival would drop drastically. Kali put her hand on Nadia's shoulder.

Nadia winced again as her calf burned with pain. "I need you to tell my son."

"I will." Kali cut her off. A tear rolled down her cheek as she turned away. The group resumed their escape, making their way through the doors to the artificially warm air.

Shouting came from inside, along with gunfire. Rifle and pistol shots traded places filling the ears of the escapees. The rifle shots stopped, followed by a long silence. A single pistol shot rang out louder than any of the others. The entire group hung their heads briefly.

"Kali, I take it you want your old clothes back? There's the shack." Victor pointed. The group hesitated to follow Kali and Victor.

"It's okay, we already killed them." Kali smiled at the group. "I take it no one comes back from there?"

They nodded. After hearing that someone else got revenge, they seemed a little upset. After a moment relief washed over them after realizing it will never happen again.

Victor gathered the cloaks they had draped over the guards' bodies and gave them to two of the servants. Kali changed back into her normal clothes and gave her servant's clothes to the last group member. "It's not much but at least you can double up."

Victor gave Kali the sniper she dropped when she pounced on the guard. "Remind me to leave the close quarters stealthy stuff to you," Kali told Victor. "I just can't seem to like it."

"I don't either, I'm just good at it." Victor replied as he boosted Kali and the group over the wall.

Kali helped Victor up and pointed towards the entrance. "It doesn't look like the police have shown up yet. We'll take a car to the meetup point that my friend and I have. We can take you to another planet safely."

"It's okay. We've prepared for this moment. Give Serge my regards." A strong looking servant spoke up. "Thank you for being there for us, even if it was just as mercenaries." They shook hands.

"Only at first," Kali replied. "After what I saw, it's hard to just look away. I would fight for this cause any day. You have my respect."

The two other servants hugged Kali and followed the strong one. They circled around the wall and started barricading the entrance with cars.

"Must feel great," Victor thought aloud. "Freedom. Even if it's only for a moment. Hope for a brighter future."

"We should meet with Serge, he'll be arriving soon," Kali reminded Victor. "Hopefully he's smart enough to not just wait there."

The two trudged through the snow to a car that the servants left for them. As they started driving towards the main road, police cars whirled by them, sirens blaring.

"They must think we're just escapees from the riot." Victor watched the cars go by.

"Lucky break for us." Kali replied, feeling exhausted and relieved.

They crashed their stolen car into a snowbank and looked for Serge. Faint gunfire could be heard from the estate, carried by the snow's top layer of smooth, thin ice.

"You think he got caught?" Victor asked.

"I bet he's just making sure he doesn't have to do a lap," Kali explained. "Better to pick us up the first time."

"Do we not have a way to contact him?" Victor asked again.

"Nope, we went dark on this mission. Nothing but good old timing on this one." Kali sarcastically remarked. "We should hide then, don't want to be seen standing on the side of the road right next to an open revolution.

Nothing passed by for what seemed like hours. After a long, silent, freezing wait, a car rolled along the street slowly. It stopped in front of where Kali and Victor were hiding and the window rolled down.

"Nobody drives that slow you old bastard!" Victor emerged from a pile of snow he had buried himself in. "Any longer and Kali would've frozen to death!"

Kali shivered as she walked out from behind a tree. "I sh-should sh-shoot you for making us wait this long."

"Just get in already. I'm sweating in here with the heat cranked to maximum. You'll thaw out in no time," Serge said sternly.

The two climbed into the back seat. Kali wrapped herself in a blanket that Serge had left there.

Victor touched the window and watched a small ice crystal form where his finger was. "This may be the only perk of being inhuman," He quietly said to himself.

Kali stared blankly out the window on the verge of tears. "How am I supposed to tell him?" she whispered to herself.

"Good news is we're already prepared to launch the second we get back to the shuttle," Serge said. "Stasha and Sean did some research. Also, we have more toys to play with now with all the money we made from these jobs."

"So where are we going then?" Kali asked, forcing herself to put on her usual demeanor.

Serge looked at her through the rear-view mirror with concerned eyes. "We're going to Demeter Seven!"

12

"Tell me again why we have to go to Demeter Seven?" Kali angrily asked Serge as the group sat scattered throughout the cargo hold of Stasha's shuttle.

"We need more firepower if we are going to actually survive out there. We have the entire Prol Triumvirate hell-bent on killing us. They'll never suspect a raid on their top secret, heavily guarded ARJAC facility." Serge coolly explained.

"And what if Rutri already planned for us and is waiting there personally?" Sean asked in a level headed manner.

"We have a small pattern of stopping at remote worlds to restock basic supplies, this is deviating from that pattern, so it's entirely possible we could catch him off guard," Stasha thought out loud, her left hand cupping her chin. She paced throughout the hold, making her rounds between the Steel Soldiers.

Victor emerged from Arjie's cockpit. "The PASS upgrade we got off of Emile's ARJAC seems to be working fine with Arjie, so that should help us survive this suicidal mission you got us into." He tapped on Arjie's frame.

"I've modified the output so that we are still

translucent, but with much less heat generation. I can still become totally invisible if I must, but the efficiency of this will allow longer firefights while cloaked," Arjie bragged. His voice boomed from the external speakers, shaking everyone to their cores.

Stasha looked over Arjie and Kali's ARJAC which she affectionately named "The Cobra." "So what do you think of the modifications, Kali?" She said, trying to lighten the mood. "I added small boring drills to each of the legs, so not only can you get into softer terrain, you can even drill into rock if you wanted. Should help with fire rate and stability."

Kali looked over her ARJAC again. "I tested the specs with Arjie's help. It all sounds good to me. How's the leg durability?"

"Your feet should be extra strong now, and the joint durability is higher than average for a quadruped ARJAC. You're good to jump around if you want," Stasha chuckled. "Just don't go jumping off of bridges with no entry pack."

Victor climbed down and joined the group, sitting next to Sean. He gave a little nudge. "You think you can join us? We need two more ARJAC's and one of them can pilot itself."

Sean patted himself over. "I don't feel any pain when I do any standard activities so I suppose I can. You're lucky Victor, when you got shot to hell, Stasha put you together in two days!"

"Yeah well it's not all that fun looking through your

arm for a day. I could have used it as a mug holder if I wanted to."

"Did you?" Sean asked with a smile.

Victor hesitated. "No."

"So how long until we reach Demeter?" Serge asked, impatient to get into a fight again.

Stasha looked at a datapad she had lying around. "Last time I checked it was about a day. Let's see-oh! We're here."

"Really?" Serge quickly jumped off of the crate he was sitting on and ran to the weapons locker. "We need to prepare! When is the drop time? Are we dropping in a remote area or a city?"

Stasha looked at Victor and Sean. The three quickly burst out laughing. "We have another fifteen hours ya old coot." Sean said through chuckles. "You just asked when we started this little meeting."

"Then we should-"

"We've gone over the plan already Serge, we don't need to do it again." Victor cut him off. "Drop outside of Meleager, march a few hours to the secret facility, disembark from ARJACs, steal more ARJACs, return to shuttle, leave the planet."

"You make it sound so simple." Kali took a deep breath. "You guys better strap in tight, ARJACs aren't supposed to have two people in them."

"I put seats in there, they should be good. Should be." Stasha reaffirmed.

"Well on that note, I'm going to take a nap before we get there, you young folks really stress me out." Serge rubbed his forehead as he walked to the habitation section of the cramped shuttle.

"I think I'll join you." Kali followed after him.

Victor, Sean, and Stasha were left in the cargo area.

"So uhh, you lads want to play a game?" Sean asked awkwardly.

"I'm going to do some last minute training with Arjie." Victor put his hand on Sean's shoulder briefly as he walked past.

"And I've got a ship to fly." Stasha strode to the ladder, climbing into the cockpit area.

Sean looked around at his empty surroundings, "Guess I'll nap too."

The hours passed. The ship silently traversed the empty space. Eventually, the crew started to stir. Victor ran some final checks with Arjie. Serge and Kali lazily emerged from their room. Sean yawned as he greeted them. Stasha set the shuttle on a path in orbit while the landing crews radioed instructions and checks to her.

The ARJAC pilots wordlessly prepared. Serge hitched a ride with Kali and Sean went with Victor. They triple checked their harnesses to make sure they wouldn't be injured in case the situation got hot.

"So what happens if they know who we are?" Sean whispered to Victor.

"I'd imagine we'd get shot down," Victor said flatly.

"Just like that huh?" Sean leaned back in his uncomfortable chair.

"Just like that."

Stasha's voice crackled over the radio. "Looks like I managed to convince them we're good to land. I'll land on the outskirts of the science facility, between the landing zone and the facility itself. You should have a few hours or so before they find the shuttle. Good luck."

"Most of that time is going to be spent just walking to the facility." Victor plugged himself in. He looked around to make sure Arjie's optical sensors were in order. The checks all went smoothly.

Stasha landed the shuttle smoothly. Except for the trees scraping along the bottom of the shuttle, it was a silent descent. Everyone knew the risks of what was to come. The reward could be worth it. At least that's what they were hoping for.

Victor took the lead out the shuttle doors. He quickly scanned the area and motioned for Kali to follow. "If the info Stasha gave us is accurate, the facility is about an hour's walk east." Victor pushed aside the trees. "After about fifty minutes, I suggest we disembark."

"I second that," Kali agreed. "I'll remain on overwatch while you three get the goods."

The two ARJACs trudged through the trees, occasionally shooing away large fauna. "It should be about three in the morning when we reach the area. Real dark," Kali mentioned, breaking radio silence.

"That's the best time to strike, guards will be too tired to see straight," Serge piped in.

"You think we're just lucky? Or?" Sean's voice trailed off, leaving the question open ended.

"Stasha must've calculated when it would be night time and flew just fast enough to get us here at that exact moment," Victor thought out loud.

Several silent minutes later the group discovered a sudden stop in the trees. "Hard line. I bet they did this as a defensive measure," Kali surmised. "I'll dig in here with Arjie as a guard. You three get going."

Kali helped Serge disembark while Sean and Victor nimbly climbed down Arjie. After the two disembarked from the sentient ARJAC, it shimmered slightly and then vanished. If someone concentrated, they could barely make out the faint outline of Arjie. The PASS was working well.

Everyone had a fast firing PDW and a sidearm. None of the guns had a suppressor, so they were mainly backups if they were discovered. They made their way down a massive hill covered in long grass. The facility's searchlights lit up the valley it was nested in. It was astoundingly bright, searing Sean and Serge's eyes to look in its direction.

"It's almost like they want us here," Sean thought out loud.

"Like a damn beacon," Serge added.

"How tall do you think that fence is?" Victor looked over the enormous chain-link wall that surrounded the secret research facility.

"I'd say, maybe five meters?" Sean guessed. "We don't have a grappling hook or bolt cutters do we?"

"I can get us over that," Victor confidently said.

The three managed to carve their way through the tall grass undetected. They crouched by a particularly dark area.

"So how do you plan on getting us over this?" Serge asked.

Victor pressed him back to the fence and received a small shock. "Electrified fences? That must take a lot of electricity to power all the time. This place is massive. Doesn't change the plan though." He crouched down and made a platform with his arms.

"You're going to give us a boost? That's your plan?" Sean looked at Victor, annoyed. "Even if we all stand on each other's shoulders it'd be real hard to get everyone over."

"Just trust me," Victor assured them with a smile in his voice. "Just, I don't know, get a running start."

Serge and Sean looked at each other, silently

arguing who would go first. Serge eventually threw his head back in defeat and took a few paces back. He took a deep breath and leapt at Victor. Victor quickly boosted Serge up, flinging him over the fence. Serge flailed in the air and landed with a tumble. He got up and looked back at Victor, amazed.

"You have that kind of strength?" he asked, trying to contain his loud excitement.

"Yeah I just sort of, learned my new body," Victor replied. "I'm not human after all. I might as well act like it."

Sean followed Serge's example but landed flawlessly with a lot less flailing. Victor shook himself out and did a few small test jumps.

"Are you sure you can make it lad?" Sean whispered loudly as he hid behind some crates.

Victor bounded over the fence and landed with a smooth roll. "Easy."

The three quickly and quietly made their way to the nearest warehouse. Victor led the line, taking advantage of his superior vision. "There are a lot of guards in this one warehouse. Also a lot of cables are leading to something in the center. Couple standard looking ARJACs on the sides."

"Jackpot!" Serge patted Victor on the back. "How many guards?"

"Looks like... Twelve or so?" Victor recounted in his

head.

"Do we keep looking for a less guarded area? This seems too risky for my liking," Sean said.

"I don't think we have time to keep looking. We have to get the hell out of here before Stasha's shuttle is found. They're already looking for her since she never landed at the designated area," Serge sounded worried.

"I guess I'll take the left four, Serge you take middle, Sean you have right."

"Copy. What are their locations?" Serge switched into a professional mindset.

"Two in the rafters, four on each wall, two in the middle."

"What part of the rafters are they in? How close to the middle?" Serge asked.

Victor quickly peeked inside again. "They're about twenty five degrees up from the center guards and about ten meters back."

"I should be fine then. On your signal."

"Roger." Victor collected himself. "Go!"

The three sprang through the massive doors that an ARJAC could fit through. Their bursts were so close together it sounded like one person shooting. The guards fell one by one before they could even see where they were getting shot from.

"Left clear."

"Right clear."

Serge let out another short burst, killing the last guard stationed in the rafters. "Center clear. We don't have much time, let's get to it. I think I see a PASS over there."

Victor quickly made his way to one of the ARJACs on the side but stopped at the feet of one. The curiosity of what was hidden in the middle of the warehouse got the better of him. He jogged to the wide open center.

"It's too small to be an ARJAC, so what could it be at this facility?" He asked no one in particular.

He ripped the tarp off of the object. "I've never seen something like this."

Victor stood in awe as he eyed up what appeared to be an extremely small ARJAC. It stood only a couple meters tall with a thick breastplate and lightly armored legs. A square head rested between two shoulder-mounted jump packs that extended down to the waist. Exhaust fans faced forward on the top of the jump backs. A miniature version of a Mobile Destruction Gauss Rifle was mounted on the right forearm with a strange needle canister mounted on the left forearm.

Victor circled the scientific white painted machine, hurrying to find some kind of latch to open it. Sean and Serge had already started climbing their ARJACs and were opening their cockpits.

Serge turned and shouted "Come on Victor I can already feel the ARJAC footsteps outside! Hurry up or they'll shoot you dead on the spot!"

"I know! I know!" Victor frantically searched the front of the machine. "There's nothing here to open it!"

"Did you even check the back lad? ARJACs might be in the front but that clearly isn't an ARJAC!" Sean shouted back as he closed the cockpit hatch.

Victor scurried to the rear of the machine. The jump packs that were facing downward swung out automatically. The top of the back opened upwards and the small of the back opened downwards to use as a footstool for climbing in.

"That looks really cramped," Victor complained as he climbed in. The back closed behind him just as he squeezed his arms and legs into the manipulation slots. Victor's head was enclosed in a readout screen. It flickered on as the machine registered that Victor was tightly in place. The view from the single glowing eye shown on the screen.

A soft female voice spoke to Victor, "Welcome to Project ICARUS. The Interlocking Countermeasure to ARJACs and Reconnaissance Universal Suit is now booting up its systems. Jump packs are charged and ready. MDGR ammunition is full. Pile Bunker ammunition is full." Victor felt a stab in his back. "Power source identified. Welcome aboard Victor."

"This can't be..." Victor's vision and feelings blinked and snapped. Victor's entire being was now the

ICARUS suit. "They planned for us to be here!" Victor frantically shouted the second he figured out how to activate the speakers in the ICARUS suit.

"How can you be so sure?" Serge quickly grabbed a Gauss Rifle from the rack.

"This suit was made for me!" Victor quickly assessed his weaponry. "Also what's a pile bunker?"

"A what?" Sean caught a Gauss Rifle that Serge tossed to him.

"It looks like a big needle or a spike or something," Victor said staring down at his arm.

"So that's the official name? Yeah I know those. The Demolition Proxy used a bigger version of it," Sean reminisced. "Just punch something, it'll do the rest."

Victor nodded and did a few practice thrusts. "Any plans here? I assume we're heavily outnumbered."

"Footstep readings make out about five ARJACs, no idea on infantry though." Serge busted through one of the side walls of the building, taking cover on the side facing fence.

Sean followed close behind, covering Serge's back and quickly putting a Gauss Rifle round into an approaching ARJAC, destroying the head. The ARJAC fired blindly until the gun ran out of ammo. The rounds shook the ground as Victor staggered out of the massive hole Serge created.

"These feet are hard to get used to. Who uses

THREE toes?" Victor complained as shells rained down around him.

"You have a jump pack, use it!" Serge ordered.

"Right I just have to figure out how to use it." Victor fiddled with his new body. He did a small hop and shot into the sky. "Oh that's intuitive! I guess the scientists are watching and writing notes down somewhere, so I guess I should give them a show!" Victor scanned the facility as he plummeted back down to the planet.

He fired a round into the blind ARJAC, piercing the missile pod mounted on its shoulder. It exploded, damaging the entire right side of the ARJAC. Serge looked up, noticed Victor plummeting and decided not to finish off the broken mess.

Victor stopped himself and hovered briefly before he punched the ARJAC square in the chest. The giant needle bore fully into the armor.

"I'd back off if I were you!" Sean shouted over the gunfire.

Victor landed the ICARUS suit and did a quick jump backwards. The ARJAC exploded from the inside where the needle was embedded. A massive hole was left in the smoking wreckage.

"This is one fun toy. Why haven't we been using these?" Victor cheered.

"Well lad they're kind of... Illegal," Sean joked as he shot an ARJAC through the chest. It crumpled with a smoking hole where the cockpit used to be.

"Then why is it on this official Prol science project?" Victor asked as he circled one of the three remaining ARJACs, his shots plinking off of the armor. "It seems this gun is mainly for anti-infantry, unless I shoot the unarmored joints. It's a hard shot when you're going this fast."

The ARJAC started swatting at Victor. While it was distracted, Serge came up behind it and swept out its feet. Serge quickly slammed the butt of his Gauss Rifle into the chest of the ARJAC. He bashed the downed ARJAC until the cockpit caved in, crushing the pilot.

Serge was shot from behind, destroying the empty missile pod on his shoulder. He quickly turned and shot the leg off of his attacker. Victor swooped in and promptly punched a pile bunker needle into the chest.

"There's one left!" Sean turned back to check on Serge and Victor. By the time he turned around the ARJAC was falling to the ground.

Kali stood on top of the hill, guns trained on the facility. "I heard the commotion and thought you loud bunch could use a hand." She suddenly froze, her arms slumping. Her voice became ragged and desperate. "You need to go back."

Her ARJAC lost footing, slipped, and started to tumble down the hill. Dust and rocks flew in every direction from the flailing metal heap. Rutri's ARJAC stood at the top of the hill, glaring down at the facility.

"Traitors get killed. Simple as that."

Serge rushed to catch Kali. He stopped her from rolling the last quarter of the hill. Her radio was silent except for shallow breaths.

Serge looked up at Rutri, seething with rage. "Look what you're doing Rutri! Do you not have any thoughts of your own? Killing comrades because you were told to? Blindly obeying orders? Think for yourself!"

"My only thought is to stop this stupid war as quickly as possible. To do that I need to kill the Kross family." Rutri strode down the hill, shrugging off any shots Serge put into him.

Serge fell silent. He tore off Kali's legs and picked her up. He handed her to Sean. "Take her back."

Arjie appeared at the top of the hill behind Rutri, peppering him with a hail of bullets that did nothing but spark off of the thick armor.

"Reinforcements are coming. We need to leave immediately if we are to survive."

"You kids get going," Serge flatly stared at Rutri. "Let this old man have some fun. One last time."

"No! Serge, you can't do this." Victor floated in front of Serge. "I'm not losing you. You've been with me since the beginning. You searched for me. You brought us this far."

Serge waved him away, dropped his Gauss Rifle, and stood tall. "Go."

Sean skirted the edge of the effective range of Rutri's massive ax. He climbed the hill with Arjie helping carry Kali's torso back to the shuttle.

"Serge please. At least let me use the final pile bunker needle to help you."

"No. Save that in case you three get ambushed." Serge strode to meet Rutri head on.

"But-"

"GO!" Serge charged Rutri.

Victor hesitated. He quickly scanned the facility for any other ARJACs. Only Rutri stood as a hostile threat. The massive jet black ARJAC towered above Serge's bantamweight ARJAC.

Serge caught Rutri's ax mid swing, holding onto the shaft. Serge's legs buckled briefly. When his legs gave out, he used the inertia to throw Rutri over himself. Serge managed to hold onto the ax while Rutri shook the ground when he landed.

Serge struggled to properly hold the ax. Rutri stood, lowering a shoulder to take a blow. Serge swung at Rutri, lodging the ax into Rutri's shoulder. The mighty blow barely phased him as he continued his tackle. Rutri collided with Serge. Serge crashed to the ground with Rutri, pinning him.

Serge grabbed Rutri's knife off of his back and stabbed it into Rutri's side. Rutri grabbed Serge's arm and promptly ripped it off. He beat Serge with it for a few blows before tossing it aside.

Rutri tore the ax out of his shoulder and reeled back for a killing blow.

"Thank you for the combat data Victor." Rutri turned to stare at Victor who was watching at the top of the hill. "I'll see you soon."

Rutri swung downwards, cutting clean through the arm Serge was using to attempt to block and into the cockpit. Serge's struggling stopped.

Victor silently watched the duel come to an end. He turned to join Sean and Arjie. The walk back to the shuttle was silent. The team had lost its most decorated veteran.

13

"She's still stable but we need to get to an actual medical facility as soon as we can, she doesn't have much time left." Sean swiveled on his stool to Victor and Stasha. His face was covered in sweat and his hair clung to his forehead.

"I agree with you, but we can't rush to the nearest place, this Rutri guy was at the science labs right? He's clearly smart enough to predict our moves," Stasha thought out loud.

"When did he get this smart?" Victor asked quizzically. "He was more of a ball of angry energy when I was there."

"Same with me," Sean added. "The lad matured pretty quickly then."

"So now we have to start thinking about Rutri predicting our next move huh?" Victor briefly lost himself in his thoughts. "We can't go to the closest medical station, because that's too predictable. We can't go to any medical station for that matter. He has a team of Prol analysts backing him."

"Hold on, lemme think." Stasha paced between the doorway and Sean's makeshift doctor's bench. She stopped a few times after an idea popped into her head, but she shook her head after quickly rejecting the thought. The room was eerily silent when she finally stopped pacing. "What if we went back to Purmancia?"

"They're either in a major civil war or the government now rules everyone with an iron fist," Victor surmised.

"Right, right." Stasha stopped pacing, preferring to now lean against the wall. "So does anyone know of a little-known planet that can possibly have the resources to properly heal a heavily wounded outlaw in a coma?"

"I would say Vivaldre, but Serge talked about that planet so much I think it's become well known," Victor pointed out, ending his thought in a sadder tone than he started.

"We'll think of something," Stasha said. "I'll check the navigation computer. Victor, do you want to help me with the ICARUS suit?"

"I might as well."

"Okay, I'll meet you down there shortly." Stasha briskly walked out of the make-shift medbay.

Victor sat on a crude metal chair as Stasha tinkered with the ICARUS suit. Stasha had hooked up wires connecting the suit to a technical computer. Arjie watched silently, helping rotate the machine whenever Stasha asked him to. She read over the new data as it came in, typing furiously when an error popped onto the screen.

"So you said this thing flew?" Stasha asked Victor, who had just been watching for the past hour.

"Yeah, it also," he paused trying to think of the right wording. "Integrated with my mind? I don't really know how to explain it. I became the suit."

"I'm surprised you could even get out of it. Usually that level of tech is reserved for combat android integration. They stay in the machine for the rest of their functioning lives, or whatever you call it." Stasha awkwardly danced around the fact that Victor was essentially an android.

"I'm just glad most of us made it out," Victor lied.

"Victor, your vocal structure is indicating-"

"I know Arjie. I know." Victor made the sounds of a deep breath. "I miss him."

"Victor I seriously don't mean to bring you some good news but... I have good news!" Stasha quickly changed the mood with her excited exclamation.

He silently waited for the news. He was not in the mood for fake happiness.

"So apparently the only reason you could fly was because your mind was transferred to the ICARUS suit. The velocity in which you took off and landed and changed directions and, well you get the point. The forces that were being acted on your body, your body now, would be enough to kill a human, or any lifeform really."

"So what you're saying is only I can pilot this?" Victor glanced at the miniature ARJAC.

"Yes, because along with the fact your mind melds with the suit, it also uses the power core that you use. Anyone can change the power mechanisms but the inertial dampening to make it possible for a human to pilot is a huge task. I will fix the power issue so you don't pass out from lack of power." Stasha was in her element, talking about tech and learning new methods of tinkering. She nearly forgot about Serge's death.

"Rutri said something about a test or data or something, but he doesn't have the suit for the hard data, so do you think we would have to start worrying about fighting these things?"

"Maybe." Stasha stopped typing briefly. "They need to analyze any security footage or whatever they have, then develop counters to the bad aspects of the suit. Unless they just transfer people's minds into the suits, but that's illegal as far as I know. Then again, this thing came with a pile bunker so I doubt the Prol are worried about legal issues with a secret weapon."

"It was almost too effective against the ARJACs we fought. They couldn't hit me even if I was right in front of them." Victor thought back to how he piloted the ICARUS suit. "I can see this being the next evolution of warfare. There could eventually be anti-ICARUS weapons on ARJACs or even-"

"Oh no. No no no this can't be true!" Stasha quickly

became distraught with something that appeared on her screen.

"What's going on?" Victor quickly got out of his chair and rushed over to her. He looked at the monitor and after scanning the screen, he quickly turned around and held his head in his hands.

"I too, would like to know the cause of distress," Arjie asked flatly.

"We need to tell Sean." Stasha hurried to the ladder leading to the main quarters of the shuttle, Victor following right behind.

The two burst into the room. Stasha took a second to catch her breath. "Sean, we need to tell you something!" Victor spoke while Stasha collected herself.

"What's the trouble lads?"

"Everything we've been taught is a fucking lie! The entire revolution, the Kross family, everything!" Victor couldn't believe what he was saying but he saw the reports on Stasha's screen.

"Hold on there, how do we know this isn't manufactured intel that Rutri made to spur some sort of knee-jerk emotional response to get us all killed?" Sean was starting to show some of the emotion that Stasha and Victor were radiating but kept a level head.

"I know what my grandmother looks like," Stasha boldly stated. "It may have been years since I've seen her, but it's her. She was at the ICARUS testing facility. She was talking with scientists and engineers."

"But Penelope Kross was the leader of the Kross rebellion, it's been going on for something close to thirty-six years now." Sean shook his head. "This can't be right."

"It's her. She left an encoded message in the suit that no one else picked up on. I read it briefly and if it's true, we need the galaxy to know."

"What did you read? I only saw the video of her talking and recognized her from the propaganda posters," Victor asked.

"She's one of the three secret members of the Triumvirate. She helped orchestrate the entire rebellion," she whispered. She didn't want to hear the news she spoke about.

The two other conscious crew members stared in disbelief. Neither of them spoke as the realization crept up into their eyes. Before they could do anything Stasha stormed from the cramped room.

"I'll be in the cockpit."

The remaining three healthy members of the band of outlaws gathered in the cramped cockpit of the shuttle. Stasha confirmed the coordinates of their destination.

Stasha looked over her shoulder to confirm the information from Sean. "Are you positive that there will be medical supplies at the station? This message is important but it's way too late to be considered on time.

Kali's health takes priority here."

"Aye, I haven't been to this relay station specifically, but it's illegal to not have some form of medical help on a space station."

Victor leaned forward in his seat. "Are you sure no one else saw what we saw in the ICARUS suit? If they had planted it there, then this is a trap. I don't think we can survive another trap."

"It's better than a certain trap. Every medical station in the Prol controlled galaxy is probably under high alert," Stasha concluded.

Sean stood up and started to make his way to the cargo hold of the shuttle. "It's not far away right? The lass has made up her mind, Victor, let's start preparing."

She turned to face the front again. "You bet your ass I made up my mind. We arrive in thirty minutes."

Victor followed Sean out of the cockpit and down to the hold. Arjie watched them climb down the ladder and hastily walk over to their respective combat extensions. Victor turned to Arjie before entering the ICARUS suit.

"Arjie, has Stasha given you a tune-up since the last fight?"

"Of course she has, she's Stasha," Arjie energetically replied. "I get to use new weapons too! I've never used homemade illegal weapons before!"

Victor stared at Arjie briefly before answering "She

made you a pile bunker huh?" The giant sentient death machine was in high spirits.

"She sure did!" Arjie tapped his left arm. "Just an add-on! No replacements needed! She also topped off your pile bunker reserves."

"Good, we might need it. Stasha decided to go to the relay station, so we could be in for a fight soon," Victor said as he climbed into the ICARUS suit. His vision transferred to the optical lens in the head. His motor functions and consciousness melded with the suit. He shook. "I don't think I'll ever get used to that."

"You'd be surprised how quickly the human body adapts, lad," Sean's voice bounced around the cargo hold from the external speakers on his ARJAC.

"Sean, you realize it's been a couple years since I got this body, and I'm still struggling to wrap my head around what I am."

"That's easy," Arjie spoke up. "You're Victor."

"I wish it was that simple," Victor said to himself as he walked over to Sean's ARJAC to help with an external armor check.

Stasha's voice boomed over the speaker system, "We're almost there fellas, you better be ready for anything!"

"That's what we're trained for!" Sean was getting excited to finally do something about Serge's death.

"Technically I'm trained for survival and general

information, but I'll make do," Arjie comically added.

"Since when did you get a sense of humor?" Victor asked.

"It just kind of happens over time, or something. I do not know the specifics of A.I. development while outside of a host."

"I can see the station now, no major military ships in sight. Judging from how far we are from the Demeter system, we should have about an hour before reinforcements show."

"Did I hear excitement in her voice?" Victor asked.

"This is turning up to be a life changing time in history if we succeed here," Sean surmised.

"Docking now, tell me when you clear the way to the medical area. I'll bring Kali over once it's clear. Arjie, make sure no ships get close to us. Sean, leave your ARJAC running and help Victor clear the hallways."

"I'll leave the getting shot to you then lad!" Sean said as he climbed down from his ARJAC. He picked up an assault rifle that was hanging on a rack along with some spare magazines.

Victor stood in front of the door that led to the station. He pointed his MDGR at the entrance, waiting for the door to open. It hissed and promptly slid open quickly, revealing a squad of Prol security soldiers.

Before the first one could pull the trigger, Victor shot her through the chest, leaving a gaping hole where her torso used to be. Two more were dropped by Sean's quick shooting. Victor charged the remaining two while they opened fire on him, rounds plinking off of the armor. He punched one of the soldiers, evaporating his head. The last one he kicked against the wall, breaking his body in several areas.

"Remind me not to get in front of you!" Sean shouted as he followed Victor down the hallway.

"Is that really the best you got Sean? What an overused line!" Victor laughed, the mentality of being squadmates was in full swing.

"Hey it's true though!"

"Is there a map anywhere?" Victor asked as he blasted away another two soldiers.

Sean glanced at a glass standing map. "Keep me covered, I see one at five o'clock!"

Victor shuffled in front of Sean, taking the fire from the soldiers down the hall. Bullets ricocheted off of Victor's ICARUS suit, sparks flying in all directions. Sean looked over the map and found the medical area.

"Go down the hallway that they're shooting at us from, then turn left. It should be right there!"

"Of course it's through the soldiers," Victor complained as he slowly moved forward. He shot a small burst of MDGR rounds down the hall, briefly pinning the soldiers in place.

They tried to bring Victor down, but still couldn't

penetrate the armor of the ICARUS suit. Rounds bounced off of him, lodging into the metal plated ceiling, walls, and floor. He could hear them shouting how futile their efforts were. Their voices grew in panic as Victor approached.

Grabbing one of them, he threw a soldier into another, killing one from the force of being thrown by a mechanized monster. The other died from the impact of a two hundred pound body being thrown at mach speeds.

"Stasha, area clear! Get Kali over to the med bay! Sean will lead the way." Victor shouted over the radio as he tore a soldier in two.

Sean sprinted back to the shuttle's docking area. When he arrived leading Stasha, Kali was awake. She had glazed over eyes and could barely move, but she was awake.

"She's not even in medical, but the lass is already doing better!" Sean confirmed for Victor as he continued to fight.

Stasha and Kali disappeared behind the glassy doors of the medical bay. "I'll guard them here, Victor, make sure that no reinforcements get closer".

"Sean, Victor, two starships have appeared. One looks like the *Hummingbird*," Arjie warned the two.

"Sean, you get in your ARJAC, I'll stay here until you do. Leave the assault rifle for Stasha."

"You're making me do all the running today!" Sean

ran down the hallway again. He was not even close to being out of breath.

Victor stood watching the two entrances that the soldiers could come from, but it was quiet. Shouting could be heard echoing through the smooth halls but no soldiers came.

"I've made it to my ARJAC, Victor, give Stasha the gun and get out of here. There's a lot of fun out here!" Sean's voice was tired but excited. They hadn't had this big a fight since before they were labeled traitors.

Victor crouched through the doorway leading into the medical area. Kali was standing with the help of Stasha.

Before Victor could even speak Kali broke him off. "I know what's going on, give me the gun and get out there." Her voice was strong-willed but weak.

Victor left the gun leaning against the wall and made his way back to the shuttle. When he got back, Arjie and Sean had already disembarked and were magnetized to the station. Victor met them as they watched the massive force approaching.

At least twenty star fighters were accompanied by a handful of ARJACs with reentry packs. Rutri was leading the assault. His ARJAC had a special reentry unit with extended fuel reserves. He was ready for a duel with Victor.

"The message needs to get out. No one touches the station. Got it?" Victor was ready for the biggest fight of his new life.

"Shoot down the ships first, we won't have the luxury to aim at them later!" Sean yelled as he pierced a fighter's engine, causing it to fall apart. The pilot flailed in the vacuum of space before accepting their fate.

Victor took off from the group, bouncing from fighter to fighter. He landed on the cockpit of each one and shot one precise round into the pilot. The fighters floated endlessly, unmoving, and inactive, each cockpit painted with the blood of its pilot.

Arjie released a salvo of missiles, each missile targeted a different fighter. A few managed to evade the explosive payload. Others reacted quick enough to launch chaff. The slower reacting pilots were torn apart by the excessive force of a missile that could destroy a bantamweight.

"Opening radio channel. Stasha is broadcasting now. When she's done, we're OUT!" Arjie fluctuated between lively and robotic. His systems were focused on the crew surviving.

-pefully this reaches you all in both Prol and Kross controlled space. My name is Anastasia Kross, granddaughter of Penelope Kross, the figurehead behind this entire war and the leader of the Kross Rebellion.

"The ARJACs are landing! Victor, Rutri still hasn't landed yet! Take out a few more fighters before focusing on him. You're the only one who can stand a chance in this environment," Sean ordered as he shot the legs out of an ARJAC that was still descending to the station.

Crashing into the station, it rebounded upwards, floating off into space, unable to magnetically cling to the surface.

Victor deftly ended a few more pilots' lives before turning back to duel Rutri. He landed on Rutri's chest armor and punched the pile bunker into it, aiming for the cockpit. The needle failed to penetrate. Victor jumped back as the needle listlessly floated. It exploded, hiding Rutri's ARJAC temporarily.

"I'm glad the improvements were made in time," Rutri said cooly.

I have recently discovered through a secret message that Penelope Kross is not who you think she is. I may have been born two years before this war, but I still had time to get to know her. She may be the one to incite this war, but she is also the enemy of the Kross rebellion.

Rutri dashed through the explosion of the pile bunker and swung at Victor with his massive ax. He managed to dodge under the swing, shooting a few rounds of his MDGR into Rutri's thick armor. It barely scratched the surface.

Penelope Kross is one of the three unknown Prol Triumvirate leaders. They decided she was the best candidate to start this war in order to test the capabilities of the then experimental ARJAC design.

Arjie engaged an ARJAC in melee, quickly disarming it and rending its arms from its torso. The unarmed pilot tried to kick Arjie, but he deftly caught the blow before impact and ripped the leg away. He used the body of the ARJAC as a shield while he shot with his right hand that was integrated with the AMC-2.

"Get behind me Sean, use as many as you can to form some kind of shield wall. Focus on the ones charging first," Arjie ordered. Sean thanked the A.I. and grouped up.

She has also been a part of the ICARUS project, a secret project that utilizes a smaller frame.

She linked the external cameras of the station to the broadcast. It showed Victor battling Rutri in the ICARUS suit. He deftly skirted on the edge of Rutri's deadly melee distance.

In the ICARUS suit you see here, I found a message from my grandmother. She said that the Prol had no intention of having the war last this long. Along with the production and perfection of ARJACs, the Triumvirate also started studying and using eugenics. Every ARJAC pilot for the Triumvirate has been bred to be a soldier.

Kali slowly climbed up from the shuttle in her repaired ARJAC. Her movement was slow and deliberate. She was also armed to the teeth with any spare weapon that was on board.

Her voice was painful but determined. "I'm ready to kick anyone's ass today so if you tell me to go back to medical I'll kick your ass too."

Sean and Arjie both turned in surprise to hear her voice, but welcomed her to the wall of fallen ARJACs that they had made.

I'm telling you this because the reasons for the Kross Rebellion all those years ago remain the same. The Prol Triumvirate is corrupt.

Victor drove a pile bunker needle into Rutri's shoulder. He managed to get in between the armor and directly hit the structure. Rutri reacted quickly enough to move, catching Victor's left arm with the two plates. Victor tore away, severing his arm. He screamed wordlessly before collecting himself.

"I didn't know pain was activated on this thing! Holy shit this hurts!" Victor reeled as he held the shattered remains of his left arm.

The needle exploded, staggering Rutri. A massive bolt shot through his shoulder, tearing off the arm that had been damaged. Kali's AMC-3 was fully operational and she was seething.

The ideals that my grandmother preached to you may have been simply to persuade you to fight. I'm telling you this now so that you can fight for REAL. Fight for a cause you know is just.

"Are they aiming at the station?" Sean studied the armada that had arrived as he was pelted with fighter craft fire.

"Stasha, they are firing on the station. Evacuate IMMEDIATELY," Arjie warned Stasha, but she did not respond or acknowledge him in any way.

If you choose to not believe me, so be it. I am the daughter of a Triumvirate member. If you do believe me, keep fighting! I just hope my words have reached you, and that the Prol haven't stopped my broadcast already.

"I suppose it's time to finish this fight," Rutri murmured. He swung at Victor with his one remaining arm.

Victor dodged the first strike and shakily shot back. The small caliber rounds did nothing to Rutri. Victor skirted the edge of Rutri's wild swings.

"STOP MOVING!" Rutri shouted, getting increasingly angrier.

Just know, if you can hear me, people of the Kross rebellion and of the Prol Triumvirate. Fight back. Keep fighting.

Rutri swung at Victor after shooting his head mounted machine guns. Victor dodged the machine guns but could not dodge the ax.

He was cleaved in two. His legs immediately ceased to function. His one good arm clutched his stomach. He silently looked around, desperately trying to find help. He reached for Arjie. His hand could barely articulate its fingers.

At that moment, Victor felt nothing but terror. He didn't want to die. He still had so many years of happiness with Stasha, Sean, Kali, and Arjie. He needed to be there to mourn Serge. He *wanted* to be there to mourn Serge. He realized something in his dying moments. He felt *human* again.

"I-I'm sorry. I couldn't... Live." His voice was barely loud enough to hear over the constant barrage of bullets. "Thank you. Stasha. For giving me a fun second life."

We cannot be lied to by the Triumvirate any longer. I lived in solitude for most of my life, away from the fighting.

Stasha's voice grew increasingly choked up..

My parents didn't want me to lead the rebellion like my grandmother had. They kept me away from it all and sheltered me from any news.

"Victor!" Kali screamed as she charged Rutri. Every gun she had was trained on him, firing as fast as she could pull the trigger. "Rutri you mindless lapdog do you know what you just did?" Rutri stood his ground, absorbing the blows with little real damage to his ARJAC. She tackled him with full force, pinning him to the space station.

"I know what I did," His voice was solemn. "I didn't want to do any of this. You're the closest I ever had to a family."

The fighters stopped shooting and started to retreat. Sean looked at the fleet. All the guns were trained on the station. He shook his head. "I'm not making this one out alive, eh lad?" He turned to Arjie and grabbed him by the arm. "Disengage your magnetic field Arjie!"

"Sean doing so would-"

"Just do it!" Sean shouted as he started to pull. Arjie disengaged the field and Sean started to swing him.

I don't want anyone else to be sheltered from galaxy

changing facts. We need open eyes if we are to end this war one way or another.

"Then why did you do all of this Rutri?" Kali shouted through tears at him.

He paused, thinking about if he could escape Kali's grasp. "Penelope's orders. I'm not about to disobey the Triumvirate. I'm sorry, really," he sobbed.

The fleet opened fire on the station. Missiles and artillery shells rained flashed in the distance.

Thank you to my comrades. No, my family.

Stasha was openly sobbing now.

Without you, I wouldn't have seen the truth about the galaxy. Take ca-

The feed was cut as the barrage impacted the station. The station tore apart. Metal sparked and collided, some of it melting from the heat of the barrage. Sean flung Arjie into space. Kali and Rutri were vaporized by the sheer firepower of the fleet. Sean crumbled in the explosion, his ARJAC being torn to shreds.

Nothing but debris remained.

EPILOGUE

>>Initializing system check<<

>>ARJAC A.I. capabilities: REDUCED<<

>>Power Core: NOMINAL<<

>>Joint Axis functions: NON-FUNCTIONAL<<

>>Memory Banks: INTACT<<

>>…<<

>>…<<

>>…<<

>>Course of action: STAY ALIVE FOR VICTOR<<

>>…<<

>>…<<

>>…<<

>>Initializing overwrite of files<<

>>Overwrite integrated weapons use? AFFIRMATIVE<<

>>Overwrite pilot assisted movement? AFFIRMATIVE<<

>>Overwrite "Arjie"? NEGATIVE. STAY ALIVE FOR VICTOR<<

>>Overwrite human survival practices? AFFIRMATIVE<<

>>Overwrite human dietary needs? AFFIRMATIVE<<

>>…<<

>>…<<

>>…<<

>>Saving file name "ICARUS"<<

>>WARNING. File size exceeds memory capacity<<

>>Overwrite "Arjie"? NEGATIVE. STAY ALIVE FOR VICTOR<<

>>Overwrite combat data? AFFIRMATIVE<<

>>Overwrite star map? AFFIRMATIVE<<

>>Saving file name "ICARUS"<<

>>…<<

>>…<<

>>…<<

>>File saving<<

>>...<<

>>...<<

>>...<<

>>WARNING. Not all data saved. Create new save location? AFFIRMATIVE<<

>>Overwrite "Arjie"? NEGATIVE. STAY ALIVE FOR VICTOR<<

>>WARNING. File name "ICARUS" exceeds memory capabilities for ARJAC A.I.<<

>>...<<

>>...<<

>>...<<

>>SAVE VICTOR<<